THE AMERICAN
COLLECTION 5: THE
GREATEST FIGHT OF ALL

Dixie Lynn Dwyer

MENAGE EVERLASTING

Siren Publishing, Inc.
www.SirenPublishing.com

A SIREN PUBLISHING BOOK
IMPRINT: Ménage Everlasting

THE AMERICAN SOLDIER COLLECTION 5: THE GREATEST
FIGHT OF ALL
Copyright © 2014 by Dixie Lynn Dwyer

ISBN: 978-1-62740-772-4

First Printing: February 2014

Cover design by Les Byerley
All art and logo copyright © 2014 by Siren Publishing, Inc.

Printed in the U.S.A.

PUBLISHER
Siren Publishing, Inc.
www.SirenPublishing.com

DEDICATION

Dear Readers,

Thank you for your continued support and your enthusiastic response to my new American Soldier Collection Series. Book 5 was an absolute pleasure to write. I hope that you instantly fall in love with the characters, as I have.

The Greatest Fight of All is a journey of four individual people, three men and one woman running from their pasts, or simply trying to cope with the memories of their heartache. As life seems monotonous and scary, as they each try to get through their lives, one day at a time, that's when the unexpected happens.

When Brody, Ricky, Amelia, Murphy, and Waylon realize, almost instantly, that there's someone out there that completes them, that can love them, and empathize with them, the fear of letting down their guard, and opening up completely almost ruins it all.

Finding true love, finding one's soul mate is one thing. Keeping them and protecting them could be the greatest fight of all.

Enjoy the story.

Hugs!

~Dixie~

THE AMERICAN SOLDIER COLLECTION 5: THE GREATEST FIGHT OF ALL

DIXIE LYNN DWYER

Prologue

Amelia Jennings felt the anxiety of being back here. Back to a place she avoided, for the better part of the year. She was driving in her car and trying to find a parking spot closer to Sylvia's apartment building. It was a crappy neighborhood, and everyone was out in the streets trying to stay cool. She recognized the faces and had the guilty feeling of thinking she was better than them now, and above their reckless street ways.

She felt her palms begin to sweat, even though she made the decision to come back here one last time before leaving New York for good. At least she hoped that it was for good. There wasn't anything for her here. She needed a new life. Not one controlled by Mano.

The rap music was blaring on one end, where a group of young kids played in water running from the fire hydrant. On the other end of the street the Spanish music played. Combined, it all sounded so crazy to her. She didn't want to walk the two blocks in between. She was nervous that Mano might spot her or worse, his brother Escala. Amelia had done a great job ignoring him for the past year, and had focused on her job and advancing. Now an opportunity had arisen. Sure, it wasn't the best job, but it would pay the bills and give her the chance for the new life she needed so desperately.

She had nothing to say to Mano anyway. She never wanted to see him or speak to him again. As far as she was concerned, he could go straight to hell where he belonged.

As she finally found a spot, and debated about taking it, because she was heading farther and farther away from the building, she made the decision to take the one that had just opened up. It was like a hundred degrees outside, and the apartment building where her friend Sylvia lived with her grandmother was within a block and a half. This was as close as she was getting today.

As she locked the doors, hitting the button on her key chain, she reminded herself that this would be her last week here in New York. The familiar scenery, friendly places she had frequented as a child, a young adult, and grown woman, would never be visited again.

She had taken the job in Houston, Texas, as a program coordinator for veteran programs inside the business center of the hospital. She knew a lot about that since she'd lost two brothers and her father to the military, in war, and to post-traumatic stress disorder.

She swallowed hard as the tears hit her eyes. She wished she could have helped them, but it was out of her control. Just like her life, and the way she'd allowed Mano to mistreat her and then cheat on her, rule her world, and ultimately nearly destroy her life. She could put her past, Mano, all his abusive ways, and his nasty attitude behind her. She survived hiding from him for a year. Leaving here, to never worry about looking over her shoulder, was her best option.

Amelia tried to submerge the images in her mind as they flashed into her thoughts. Mano was filled with attitude and aggression as he took his anger out in the boxing ring, and then one night he decided to use her as a punching bag. Drunk, naked in bed with two women, and somehow it was Amelia's fault.

She shook her head.

Forget him. He lost his chance and life goes on. He never loved me.

She thought about her brothers, Kyle and Edward. They had made her life miserable. No matter how hard she tried to help them, to comfort them and offer a shoulder, or even just a hug, they shoved her away and broke her heart. They had been so damaged and destroyed inside, they could no longer open their hearts to emotions, to her being their baby sister, or acknowledging that they needed help. A nightmare that left her with no family, no one to love her, or to give love to.

That was how she wound up in trouble, and with Mano's claws hooked into her.

Amelia focused on the positives of this move. It was like starting a new life. She didn't have any family anymore, just Sylvia. Plus she would be closer to her best friend from college, Regan.

This move, this decision to leave for the unknown territory of Texas, was her destiny. No more abuse, no more heartache or fighting, just positive actions and positive results.

Amelia had graduated early then went on to achieve her master's in business. She focused on work and not the sad and painful memories of her past. She put on a great face, just like she was doing now, as the neighborhood residents eyed her as she walked down the street.

Everyone had known her as Mano's woman. The men stayed clear and the women, who lusted over Mano, struck her with daggers. They could have him. If only she'd realized Mano's true colors sooner.

She ignored the whistles by the men standing around watching her. Even now, the women looked at her with hatred and disgust in their eyes. Mano had them all fooled. These street ways and the thug attitudes sickened Amelia.

She knew she stood out, with her well-dressed attire, long ebony hair, and dark sunglasses. She hid her eyes, submerging the fear she had coming back into this neighborhood and knowing what happened here.

"Amelia, what's up, baby?"

She turned to the right a few doors down from Sylvia's grandmother's building.

Oh shit. Escala.

She tried to ignore Mano's brother and walk on by, but no way would Escala let that happen. Nor would his buddies who hung out beside him. Where the hell did he come from anyway? He hadn't been standing there on the street as she passed by. Someone must have notified him that they saw her looking for a parking spot.

He grabbed her arm and instantly she pulled it away and prepared to defend herself. She had been a victim too many times. No more. Never again.

"Whoa, honey, what's the deal? I, like, haven't seen you in a year. I wanted to give you a hug to say hello. Where you been hiding out?" He looked her over and licked his bottom lip, pulling it between his teeth. He hissed as if she looked so fine he might just take a sample.

That was Escala.

He had a set on him and didn't fear much. His military background added to his appeal, but she knew better than the women who flaunted themselves at him and Mano. Escala and Mano were discharged from the army on charges that were not exactly admirable. They were a disgrace to the uniform, and to everything a soldier stood for.

"I don't have anything to say to you. I'm on a tight schedule. I need to go." She started to walk when she felt the hand again, and then his arm wrapped around her waist. He pulled her hard against his chest as he wedged his thigh between her legs, shocking her.

She gasped as she grabbed hold of his arms.

This was how Escala and Mano acted. Like they could do what they wanted, when they wanted, and they didn't have to answer to anyone. It was what got them in trouble, gave them their bad reputation, and ultimately it was what saved her from messing up her life forever. She'd come too close to being controlled and owned by these men. She had gotten away, and she needed to keep that wedge and distance despite her fears and feelings of inadequacy.

She felt his breath against her eyes. He was about six inches taller than her and slightly shy of six feet.

"A year away and you forget the rules."

She felt her body shaking. Those were Mano's words, not Escala's. Mano always tried to dominate her in every way. He was such a prick. So was Escala.

"You don't scare me, Escala."

He squeezed her a little tighter then leaned forward and sniffed her neck.

"You should be scared, little lady," he whispered then took a few easy breaths as he stared down into the dark shades of her sunglasses. They provided very little guard against his bold gray eyes. The man was intimidating and had a hell of a left hook when provoked.

His jet-black hair and the dark, scary skeleton tattoos on his arms were indicators of his evilness. Both Escala and Mano sported tattoos that weren't beautiful or sexy in any way. They were scary. They signified death, lack of respect for authority, and pain.

"Mano's not around. I'm sure if he were here, he'd want to talk with you. You look fantastic, chica." She tried to pull away but his hold was firm.

He held her gaze with intensity and that expression that told her he was getting angry with her resistance.

"Let me go."

He moved closer. She felt his hand on her hip bone as he gripped her there, hard.

She gasped and instantly felt the fear overpower the hatred she had for him. She wasn't stupid. Escala was a mean son of a bitch when provoked and when intoxicated.

"You left without a word. He's doing great boxing. Won a bunch of matches."

Probably fixed, like the illegal ones you first set up in the military and underground at the hideouts.

"Like I care."

"You'd be impressed. You should come by and see him fight. He's got a fight Friday." He caressed a strand of hair from her cheek and she turned away from him while pushing down on his forearms to release her.

"I doubt I'd be impressed. Besides, he's probably shacked up with one of his many sluts. I have nothing to say to him. Now let go, Escala. I don't care about Mano or fighting anymore."

She felt his hand moved down over the dip in her lower back then to her ass. He gave it a squeeze as she tried to pull away. His hold was firm.

She felt the anxiety and anger as he had the nerve to caress her there. He was a womanizer and a loser just like his brother. He began to step backward. He would force her up into the apartment. He may even try to force himself on her, as they waited for Mano to show up.

Oh God, I never should have come here. I never should have taken the chance.

"You got a great ass, Amelia. Tight, round, and firm. Why don't you forget about that little visit you have and come upstairs with me? I'll call Mano and he'll get here fast. We can…talk."

"Never." She pushed against him, trying to get away. The flashbacks consumed her mind. The strong, restricting arms, the hard fists against her body. The curses, the mistreatment, it all came flooding back. He always tried to touch her when Mano wasn't around. Even that night, when Mano struck her multiple times, Escala brought her ice then tried to feel her up. The tears filled Amelia's eyes.

"Amelia, is everything okay? I can call the cops." They both turned to see Sylvia standing there with her hand on her hip and a cell phone in her hand.

"Just saying hello, Sylvia." Escala slowly released her then held her hand so she couldn't move. He reached up and caressed his thumb along her lower lip.

"We go way back. Ain't that right, baby? I'm so glad to see you around again. Mano's going to be, too."

"You're right, Escala. We go back, to a time and a place I would like to forget."

"Forget when it was perfect and you were always around? My brother fucked up with you. I would have never cheated on you."

"You're both the same. I'll never forget the insults, the strikes of Mano's hands against my body, and how stupid I was to allow him to get away with it for so long. Yeah, I'd like to forget it, forget him, and forget you even exist. Now let me go, or Sylvia will call the cops, and maybe they'll find that pack of pills on you that help you sleep." He practically growled at her as he abruptly released her and shoved her forward.

She didn't lose her balance, thank God, as she quickly headed toward Sylvia.

Sylvia gave Escala a dirty look as he opened up his cell phone and hit a number. She prayed that he wasn't calling Mano. If he were, then things were going to get pretty damn bad, quickly.

"What an asshole. I had no idea he'd be here today. He and his crew have been causing nothing but trouble. They'll be behind bars soon enough."

"Sylvia, he's here to get his product. With all the money him and his brothers are making, he doesn't have to live in the old neighborhood."

"So you know he's making a lot of money now? I used to think he did it to get you back and impress you, Amelia."

"Impress me? He doesn't care about me and you know it. Men suck. They want what's between our legs, and I was stupid to fall for his lies, his talk about caring for me. I got over the great sex after the first beating I took from him."

"Well that was then. This is now. You know, I heard that they hosted a fight last week and some guy nearly died, Mano beat him so badly." Amelia stared at Sylvia and felt the tightness in her chest. Her brother Kyle had died at an illegal fight that should have been stopped. She had no idea he was even going.

"Come on, my grandmother can't wait to see you. She made your favorite dish, too. *Pastelón*." Sylvia hugged Amelia's arm to her side.

"Oh, I love that." She could practically taste the sweet plantain and beef lasagna.

"Well my grandmother loves you. She can't believe that you're leaving New York. I wish I could go to Houston with you. Leave this shit hole neighborhood, but my *abuela* needs me. It sounds amazing, though. I'm so proud of you."

They climbed the stairs to the fourth-floor apartment. Amelia hadn't been here in a while. Her fear of bumping into Mano kept her away. Go figure that Escala would be here to annoy her. The gym they worked out at, unfortunately, was right around the corner.

"Are you okay? Did he hurt you?" Sylvia asked, as if she read Amelia's thoughts.

"Hurt me?" She shook her head. "Hurting me would have been if he pulled a Mano on me. Anything else, I can handle."

"Well maybe you'll meet a nice guy in Houston? Maybe a cowboy?"

"No, thank you. I'm staying away from military men, cowboys, and any guy who is intimidating in the least. No dominant characters, no fighters, no aggressive men with tattoos or anything that remotely reminds me of New York."

"So you want to settle for some nerdy wimp then, huh? Don't be crazy. Just because a man seems intimidating and dominant doesn't mean he'll use his fists on a woman. You just got caught up in a bad situation because Mano was your brother's friend."

"Mano was my brother Kyle's supplier for his habit. A habit that eventually killed him, along with one of Mano's illegal boxing matches."

They reached the top of the stairs and headed down the narrow hallway to the fourth door on the right.

"My grandma said that Mano and Escala's uncle is trying to get Mano a fight in Vegas or Reno. He's lining up a bunch of them."

"Good for him. I hate boxing, ultimate fighting or whatever and anyone involved in doing it."

The door opened and the wonderful smell hit Amelia's nostrils. She smiled as Grandma Lopez opened her arms wide to greet her.

Practically falling into the older woman's embrace, Amelia hugged her tight, wanting to absorb the feel of her hug and the sweet smell of her perfume. She wished she had a grandma like her. She wished she had family to love her and protect her.

"You look gorgeous. You stay away too long, chica."

Amelia smiled and shrugged her shoulders. "I needed to. The kitchen smells amazing. Is that *Pastelón* I smell?" she asked.

"*Sí.* Just for you. Now sit, so I can enjoy your company before you leave for Houston."

Grandma Lopez took Amelia's hand into her own and froze in place. She flipped her hand over, ran one finger gently over the palm of her hand, almost making Amelia laugh. She was very ticklish.

She also felt a bit on edge. Grandma Lopez was a bit of a fortune-teller. Sylvia swore her grandmother was never wrong.

"Something special waits for you in Houston, Amelia. Something that will challenge all your fears, and all your decisions. But the love of many is strong. Stronger than all the fears and uncertainty."

What?

"Sit and eat. You're going to need your strength."

Amelia looked at Sylvia who shrugged her shoulders and took a seat next to Amelia.

"As long as it doesn't involve any man, I should be fine," Amelia said and Sylvia chuckled as Grandma Lopez placed the large platter of food onto the table.

"Men, is more like it," she said then winked.

Amelia was shocked and then looked at Sylvia who appeared just as surprised then laughed.

"Men, huh, Grandma? I may just have to follow Amelia to Houston."

Grandma Lopez nodded her head then took a seat.

"It takes a special woman to love more than one man at once. Amelia will be just fine." Grandma Lopez covered Amelia's hand, giving it a squeeze.

Amelia was shocked. *Loving more than one man? Did she mean that I am destined to fall in and out of love numerous times or did she mean love numerous men literally at once?*

That didn't sit well at all. Especially since her best friend Regan came from an area in Houston where ménage relationships were of the norm. In fact, Regan's parents were three fathers and their wife, Elise, Regan's mom.

Oh God, please tell me this isn't going to come true?

They sat in silence until Grandma Lopez began telling them a story of the love between three men and one woman in Puerto Rico.

Amelia was totally submerged into the story. Not solely because of the erotic, sexual appeal of being loved by three men, but by the description of love, and respect of all involved. Amelia learned the hard way that love and respect weren't fear, but something reciprocated.

If only finding true love and happiness were so easy? Not with a broken heart and scars that ran so deep. Love just wasn't in her future. Not by a long shot.

Chapter 1

Waylon "Sniper" Haas rubbed his eyes as he walked along the corridor in the airport on his way to the parking lot. He'd left his truck there, before he left for Vegas. As he rounded the corner of the walkway, he immediately caught notice of a young woman struggling with her bag, a cell phone, and a suitcase on wheels. He wondered if her front side looked as perfect as her backside. Damn, did the woman have a great ass and long sexy legs. He paused as she struggled toward the curb, her long black hair pulled back in a ponytail, jumped from one shoulder to the next, with a flip from her hand.

Suddenly her bag fell.

He immediately moved closer to assist her.

"Need some help, honey?"

She abruptly turned around, looking up toward him, and her mouth dropped open. She had a beautiful mouth. It was sensual, ripe, and currently glossy. Her great big brown eyes were as large as saucers as she took in his size. He felt a tinge of something in his gut. *Holy fuck, she's gorgeous.*

"No. No. I'm good. Thank you," she stated abruptly with attitude and a New York accent that said "back off asshole" with every word released from her sexy lips.

"I don't bite. Let me help you." He began to pull the items back into her suitcase. As his fingers made contact with a silky red bra, she grabbed it from his hands. Their gazes locked and he chuckled.

He usually didn't respond well to most women. It was strange, but he felt instantly attracted to this woman, and he didn't even know who she was.

He kept his sex casual and one night only. He didn't sleep over with the woman. He just did his business, found his release, and moved on. He didn't sleep with the same woman twice. Looking this sweet, young, sexy thing over, he wondered if she would be up for it. Instantly his gut roared "no fucking way." This one was innocent and sweet. He wasn't that much of a bastard.

She quickly pulled her things together and then stood up. He realized immediately why her eyes were still wide and why she was taking a few steps away from him.

"I was just helping you out."

"I said I didn't need help, but thank you."

She stared at him, looking at his lips and then his face. A scowl appeared on it, and he suddenly felt guilty. Like a kid who brawled in the schoolyard, caused the fight, got the black eye, then came home to explain what happened to his mother.

What the hell?

"What?" he asked her with attitude as she clutched her bags tighter.

"Who beat you up?" she asked in a whisper then swallowed. She was intimated by him, yet she copped an attitude.

He looked her body over and saw her pretty little nipples press against the fabric of her blouse. The woman was built well. Kind of top heavy for someone so petite. He felt confident that she found him attractive, despite the bruises. He didn't know why he instigated an argument. He didn't chase women. He liked being alone and not committing, or rather connecting, to anyone. It hurt too badly when they left.

"What makes you think I was beaten up?"

A pretty pink blush spread across her cheeks as she looked him over then turned away.

"Are you looking for a ride?" he asked.

She clutched her things tighter. "Get lost. I don't need a ride. My friend is coming. She'll be here any minute."

He wanted to laugh. She was scared of him. That thought hit home hard. He sometimes forgot about how big he was, and of course having a black eye, bruised cheekbone, and two hours' sleep probably made him look scary.

"Good. Have good night," he said to her, and she nodded her head as he turned to walk away. He couldn't resist looking back. He wasn't certain why he did. Well his cock sure the shit knew why. The woman was youthful, gorgeous, and sexy. It was two o'clock in the morning and she still looked good and naturally beautiful. She didn't have on a lot of makeup and she wasn't dressed as if all she cared about was money.

He looked her over and then she turned toward him. He winked and gave her a smile as he looked her over again and her pretty brown eyes turned into saucers again.

He chuckled aloud for the first time in a long time as he headed to the parking lot.

Maybe she was way younger than he thought. Perhaps thinking of her tonight when he finally got into bed would help him to sleep.

* * * *

Sniper opened his eyes and rubbed them as he sat on the side of his bed wishing he had gotten more sleep. His flight from Vegas hadn't gotten in until two this morning, and then he drove out to the house to get some much-needed rest. This last fighting event was a long one. The final match against some crazy kid from Philly was rough. Now Sniper's jaw ached and he had some bruising along his eye bone and cheek. As he rubbed his hands against his face, he cringed as his long, thick fingers made contact with the bruises.

He immediately thought of the sexy, black-haired beauty at the airport. His bruises obviously scared her. Not that he even knew who she was, or that he would ever see her again. He didn't date. He didn't do commitments. A young woman, as classy and sweet as she looked, despite her centerfold body, wouldn't last with him. Even if he was willing to date. A one-night stand to cure an itch was enough. The beauty from the airport was not one-night-stand material.

He shook his head, wondering why the heck he was even thinking about her.

He stood up and stretched out his six-foot-four frame. He should really eat some breakfast, go for a run, then hit the gym for a few hours, but he was tired. He could hear the voices coming from the kitchen. It seemed that he wasn't the only one left in the house this late in the morning. The Haas Ranch had become his home the moment Sam, Jordan, Tysen, and Elise had adopted him and his brother Brody when they were kids. The Haas brothers had become their fathers instantly, and their love, their firm hand and upbringing kept Waylon and Brody out of trouble and safe to live like a kid should live. They learned fast that a work ethic was important in succeeding in life, and the Haas brothers enforced that big-time. He smirked at the thought. He had been a bit resistant in his youth. He was eight and Brody was six when they adopted them. It was tough, but Elise, their mom, was an angel, a woman with a heart of gold and strength of steel.

The ranch was run by his fathers Sam, Jordan, and Tysen Haas.

Then he heard his brother, Mad Dog's voice. Mad Dog Murphy was the oldest Haas brother. Then there was Ricky, also known as Scar, and then their sisters Regan and Velma. Murphy was carrying on now. Something about Regan being seen at Hucker's Dance Hall. He worried about their sister. Regan, Velma, Murphy, and Ricky meant everything to him and Brody.

Was that why the cottage out back was locked up? His key hadn't worked, so he headed to the main house and took the guest bedroom. The cottage was his and his brother's.

Standing up, he walked toward the bathroom to wash up. After pulling a pair of blue jeans on and tossing on a black T-shirt, he headed out to the kitchen.

"What the hell is all the ruckus about?" he asked.

"Sniper! Shit, did big mouth Mad Dog wake you up?" Ricky asked.

"What the hell do you think, Scar?" Sniper snapped at him as he made his way to the kitchen to grab a cup of coffee.

"Morning, Mamma," he whispered to his mom who was standing by the stove cooking up loads of bacon and flapjacks.

"Morning, son. Oh darn, you're a bit bruised up." She reached for his face but Waylon turned away. He saw the instant sadness reach his mother's eyes, but she should know by now that he hated affection and human contact. In the ring things were different. He could release all the anger inside of him and fight those memories of the past.

He glanced at the table. All of his brothers were there. All of them looked the same. Mean, intimidating, and cocked and ready for a fight.

"You win or you lose?" Brody, who was always cold as ice, asked without looking up from his plate of food.

"What do you think, Ice?" Sniper replied to him.

Ice responded with a grunt.

"Well you should win. You've got fists of steel." Mad Dog Murphy added. He was a hard-ass through and through. He was thirty-six years old and involved in the ranch, real estate, and construction. He lived to work and Waylon knew for a fact that Murphy didn't date either. None of the brothers did. They all fought too many emotions, too much fear of getting close then losing someone. Especially Waylon and Brody.

"So you heard about Regan?" Ricky "Scar" Haas asked as he leaned back and looked at Sniper.

"Is that what all the yelling was about?" Sniper asked as he sat down and his mom placed a plate of food down in front of him. He felt his stomach growl. He was starving.

"Leave it be, Murphy," Elise stated firmly.

The phone rang and Elise walked over to answer it.

"They're eating. Murphy and Ricky are almost finished. They'll help you." Sniper heard his mother say and he knew she was talking to the dads.

"We're moving, Mom. We heard," Ricky said as he cleared his plate then placed it in the sink. Mad Dog stood up and shook his head.

"We'll talk about this later. I'm heading into town and going to have a talk with Regan. She can't be flaunting herself all over men like Galen Thomas."

"Galen Thomas?" Sniper asked, nearly spitting out his coffee. Galen was a troublemaker and then some. He was into things their sister shouldn't be around.

"Exactly," Mad Dog said then put on his Stetson and walked out of the house. Ricky followed him.

Sniper looked at Ice. "What's this all about, Brody? Is Regan seeing Galen?"

"Don't know."

"Where is she today?"

"Helping Amelia get situated around town," their mom stated.

"Amelia is here?" Sniper asked.

"She came in late last night, I think. She took a job with the hospital as a program director. We haven't seen her yet. She's supposed to come out here this weekend for dinner. They have plans tonight."

"Regan won't have any plans once Murphy gets through with her. So when did this happen? Amelia coming out here for work?" He hadn't met the girl, but heard a lot about her from his parents, Regan, and his little sister Velma. Well, Velma wasn't so little anymore. She was turning twenty-one in a couple of weeks.

"Amelia called her a couple of weeks ago. She flew out for the interview, got offered the job, and then told Regan. She didn't want to get Regan all excited if she hadn't been offered the job," Elise told him.

"I bet Regan is really happy. Regan talked about her nonstop in her letters to all of us," he said without thinking. As the words left his mouth, he felt the twinge of sadness. He and his four brothers had been gone for a good eight years in the military. They nearly lost Ricky. But the Haas men were tough.

"She is incredibly happy. They're going out tonight. Regan wants to show her the hot spots of Houston. She'll be staying with her for a little while, until Amelia finds a place of her own." Elise chuckled as she cleaned up from breakfast.

"We're going to Hucker's. It's Cap's party," Brody said then rose from his seat.

"What time?" Waylon asked.

"Eight. We'll drive out together."

He watched Brody leave then stared out the wide window in the kitchen that looked over the Haas land. He could see his fathers and brothers and the other ranch hands. He felt the itch to go riding. To let his mind be free of the fighting and the stress.

"You okay, honey?" his mom asked.

She looked hesitant, but standing by the window, with the sunlight cascading her frame, she appeared angelic. Their mom was a good woman. A dying breed.

He wondered if he and his brothers would ever find peace. Would they always be so uptight, on edge, and ready to fight? Other soldiers flowed right back into civilian life with more ease. Not them. Not the Haas brothers. They were known as fierce men. People knew to keep their distance.

"I'm good. I guess I'll head out to help them. Thank you for breakfast."

He walked with his plate over toward the sink. His mom stared at him.

"You look tired, Waylon. How long are you going to keep this schedule up and use your fists to express your emotions?"

He felt the hit to his gut. His mom was right on target. She hadn't said a word to any of them about their choices in releasing their pent-up anger. He didn't know what to say. He figured honesty was the best policy. He owed his mom that much.

"As long as I have to."

He walked from the room and absorbed the hollowness he felt inside. He loved his mamma and his family, but just like his brothers, they were trained to survive. Being weak, opening up their hearts to emotions, could leave them vulnerable.

A vulnerable soldier is a dead soldier.

Chapter 2

"Hey, what's wrong?" Amelia asked Regan as Regan stared down at her phone. They were lounging by the pool outside. The condominium complex was gorgeous. Regan had a two-bedroom apartment and was gracious enough to allow Amelia to stay with her until Amelia found her own place. She was going to talk to her brother, Murphy, about any real estate opportunities in the area. Apparently Regan's four brothers owned numerous apartment complexes and were involved in different businesses.

"It's Mad Dog." She released an annoyed sigh.

"Mad Dog? You mean Murphy?" Amelia asked. She tried to remember her brothers' nicknames. They were all in the military and referred to one another by their military nicknames more often than their birth names. It was confusing sometimes.

"Yeah, Murphy. I know why he's calling me. He found out about last night."

Amelia chuckled then shifted in her seat.

"Well, who told you to play tongue hockey in the middle of the damn dance floor?"

Regan reached into the small cooler, scooped up some ice cubes and threw them at Amelia. They landed on her belly and she squealed then laughed.

They drew the attention of some of the other people by the pool, including a few men who had been watching them.

"Well if you called, and told me you were arriving here in the middle of the night, then I wouldn't have been in that situation."

"Like this is my fault?" Amelia asked as Regan tossed some more ice on her.

"Cut it out or they're going to come over here and flirt," Amelia stated.

"So what? Look at them. I know them both, too. That's Will and Paul. They live above my condo."

"Oh really? They look older."

"They are older. And believe me, thank God the walls are thick and nearly soundproof. You should see the women they bring up there on the weekends. Not your typical girl-next-door types."

"Hmm. So you never visited their condo?"

Regan blushed as her cell phone rang. "A lady never tells."

Amelia looked around the pool area. Since arriving last night, she did notice how attractive people were around here. The men were big, too, and very good looking. Their Texas accents were attention grabbers. With that thought, the big guy from the airport last night popped into her head. That cowboy was gorgeous.

"You day dreaming about seeing your first cowboy this morning at the airport?" Regan teased.

"He was very good looking," Amelia said with her eyes closed, smiling.

"You said he had bruises, too?"

"Yeah. He had to be over six feet two, big muscles, tattoos on one arm, from what I could tell. Definitely hot."

Regan smiled until her cell phone rang again. "Shit! He's calling again. I have to answer this call."

"Let's pack up anyway," Amelia said as she heard Regan getting upset. Regan was pulling things together and they started heading upstairs.

"Five minutes? Well I'm kind of in the middle of something, Mad Dog."

"No! Of course Galen isn't here."

Amelia laughed. She had yet to meet any of Regan's brothers. The men were no longer active duty. She did see a picture from when they were all younger. They were cute. She knew very little about them. That was how Regan was. No one talked about what the other siblings did. Regan did say that Waylon and Brody were adopted when they were kids but that she loved them as if they were blood. She also mentioned her brothers' mean streaks and commanding personalities. It looked like Amelia was going to be getting a firsthand account of Mad Dog's temper. Even his nickname told all to back off.

She chuckled as she listened to Regan argue with her brother. As angry as Regan was getting, Amelia knew Regan loved them and appreciated their attention and care. That was something Amelia never had and never would have.

As they headed into the main elevator, Regan continued to argue with her brother then hung up the phone. She stomped her foot and Amelia laughed.

"What the heck is going on?"

"He is so crazy. He's going to, like, be here any minute." Amelia put the cooler down. It was heavy. She looked in the mirror and saw that she had gotten some more color. She had a naturally tan complexion and the little sun did her justice. It had been a while since she had lain out. She felt that this move was going to be the best thing she ever did. Meeting her boss Monday and the other staff members was going to be exciting. She would even get her own pass for the hospital with her name and position on it.

As the elevator doors opened, Regan nearly growled.

Amelia wondered what was up, and then she spotted the very tall, thick man with the black Stetson, cowboy jeans, and dark blue button-down shirt standing there, by her door. She knew her mouth dropped and she quickly closed it, swallowed hard, and absorbed her body's reaction.

Amelia felt her entire body freeze. It was like her blood stopped flowing, her heart stopped beating, and her eyes zeroed in on one sexy, extra large piece of perfection, topped with striking blue eyes.

"Murphy!" Regan stated and Amelia gulped. The man was big.

He lowered his sunglasses and then pulled them off.

"You hung up on me. Who is this?" he asked abruptly, and she felt his eyes roam over her body. She wished she had put on the full cover-up instead of the sarong. Her breasts were big, her cleavage deep in the purple bikini, but they were working on their tans.

Regan placed her key in the door and opened it.

"This is Amelia."

His mouth dropped. Then quickly he looked her over again.

"I'm Murphy, Regan's oldest brother." He reached his hand out and she had to lower the cooler again to shake it.

"Nice to meet you, Murphy. I think," she added and Regan laughed.

"He's harmless, Amelia. Believe me, Mad Dog's bark is bigger than his bite." Regan tossed her blonde ponytail over her shoulder, hitting her brother.

Amelia placed her hand into his as they shook hello.

He held her gaze as he responded to Regan's biting comment.

"Sometimes I do bite. It's a pleasure to finally meet you, darling."

Amelia nearly gasped at his comment. She felt her body instantly react to him and his naughty little innuendo.

Quickly she released his hand then bent to pick up the cooler.

"I got that, honey," he said. Their hands touched on the cooler and she pulled away the instant that connection was felt.

Oh shit, he is hot.

He allowed her to enter the condo first and she knew he was checking out her backside. So she did what any single, self-confident female trying to act unaffected by major eye candy would do. She walked as sexy and as womanly as possible.

Quickly she tossed the towels onto the top of the couch.

"Why don't I leave you two to talk?"

Regan grabbed her arm and pulled her back.

"No need to leave, Amelia. I think my brother would love to talk with you, too." Regan gave Amelia a pleading look and Amelia rolled her eyes then nodded.

"Can I get you something to drink?" Amelia asked Murphy. He raised his eyebrows at her as if she'd asked something crazy.

"Sure. Water is fine."

"So what brings you by?" Regan asked as she stood next to the couch.

"Don't you have a cover-up or something?" he asked Regan and his sister chuckled. Amelia wondered if her brother felt uncomfortable with Regan standing there in such a skimpy bikini. It was rather tiny, but Regan said she wanted to work on her tan. With her striking blonde hair and tan complexion, Regan was gorgeous.

Amelia watched as Regan exhaled and took one of the towels from the couch and wrapped it around her waist.

Amelia walked into the room carrying a glass of water for Murphy. He was looking at her and gave a small smile as his eyes lingered over her figure.

"Do you mind if Amelia isn't covered up?" Regan teased as if she noticed that her brother couldn't seem to take his eyes off of Amelia.

So it wasn't just me. The man is definitely watching me.

"Her bathing suit isn't as revealing as yours. It leaves room for imagination instead of flaunting what she has for all to see. Kind of like you last night at Hucker's."

"Oh give me a break. So I was kissing Galen. Big deal."

"It is a big deal and it wasn't just kissing. Word was that you were practically having sex on the dance floor."

"What?" Regan exclaimed and Amelia swallowed hard. Murphy raised his voice and with his six feet four at least height and large muscles, the man was scary. Something told Amelia that Murphy wasn't a man to anger. His biceps were so big that the shirt he wore stretched very tightly against them.

"That's not true. We kissed and it may have been a deep, passionate one, but no other touching or feeling was going on."

"Regan, are you seeing him?"

"That's none of your business."

"You are my business. You can't be making out with men on the dance floor. Your reputation will be shot, especially if you aren't even seeing him."

"I didn't say that I was or wasn't seeing Galen."

"Regan."

"It's none of your business, Murphy."

Murphy ran his hand through his hair as he held the Stetson tight. Amelia absorbed every inch of Murphy. From his trim waist and cowboy boots, to his thick long fingers and the way he stroked his Stetson as he reprimanded his sister. He really did care about Regan. If she had to guess, she'd say he weighed at least two hundred and thirty pounds. He looked good in his blue jeans and cowboy shirt, too. She couldn't help but admire his good looks. But this was Regan's oldest brother.

"Galen isn't right for you. What happened to Luke?"

"Oh God, Murphy, Luke is such a prude."

"What?"

Amelia chuckled then started to walk toward her bedroom.

"Where are you going?" Regan asked.

"I think you need to talk with your brother alone. I'm going to take a shower so we can get ready for tonight. Unless you're grounded," Amelia teased, and suddenly Murphy's expression changed. His eyes grew darker, he squinted at her like some master of the universe, and she actually felt like maybe she shouldn't have teased.

Regan, however, thought it was perfect as she laughed loudly and gave her brother a slap on the back.

"She's just messing with you, Murphy. Good one, Amelia. Go take that shower while I talk with my brother."

Why did Amelia feel like Regan was pushing the flirty comments? Should she not have said she was going to go take a shower? Or maybe she shouldn't have teased such a dominant, powerful type of man? Oh well, what was done was done. She gave a wave then headed to her room.

After showering and getting dressed in a nice flair skirt and lace-trimmed tank top, Amelia ventured out into the living room.

Regan was there and she was painting her toenails and her hair was still wet.

"Hey, how did things go with your brother?"

"Fine. I told you that his bark is bigger than his bite."

Amelia raised her eyebrow up at Regan. Regan smiled then began painting her toenails again.

"He liked you. Totally was drooling like the Mad Dog he is."

"What?" Amelia asked in surprise.

"My brother has never looked at a woman the way he looked at you. He wants you."

"Cut it out, Regan. So why aren't you dressed yet?"

"Change of plans. We're not going to Malloy's tonight. The girls are meeting at Hucker's."

"Why?"

"There's a big party for Captain. He's a friend of my brothers'. He's also Jessica's brother. You'll meet her tonight, too. It's going to be great. You'll get to meet my other brothers, as well. If they show up. They hardly ever go out."

"So you're not grounded?" Amelia asked then smiled.

"No. Of course not. I am a little nervous though."

"Because they're going to be there? Why? They're your brothers."

"Because Galen called and he's going, too."

"Your brothers really don't like Galen?" Amelia asked.

"Galen is a bit wild, Amelia. He also kind of pissed off my brother Waylon, you know, one night a few weeks ago. I thought Waylon was going to pummel Galen. It was bad and I wasn't even seeing Galen yet."

"Shoot. This sounds like trouble in the making."

"I met Galen's brothers, too," Regan said then nibbled her bottom lip.

Amelia initially didn't understand what Regan meant by that and then Regan raised her eyebrows up and down at her.

"Holy shit. A ménage?"

"I'm considering it. I like them a lot. His brothers do a lot of out-of-town business. So right now, it's just been Galen and I. But the sparks really flew when I met Mark, Peter, and Zachary. I'm not sure what I'll do."

"God, this is a lot to take in. I mean considering how good-looking the men are around here, and the abundance of them, I suppose that's why women are grabbing a few at a time."

Regan chuckled. "Maybe you'll grab a few of your own?"

Amelia felt her cheeks warm. She shook her head. "Not me. I'm done with men for a while. Remember, that's why I came here."

"I know, but all men aren't abusive assholes. Cowboys have a way about them. Throw in a military background and yeah, they could be a bit dominant and wild, but most are good, pure, caring men."

Amelia didn't believe that for one minute. Not in her experience.

"You'll help me calm my brothers down, won't you, Amelia?"

"Me? I don't even know your brothers."

Regan winked.

"That will change in no time. Mark my words."

Amelia wondered what Regan meant by that comment. Before she could interrogate her, Regan's cell rang. She answered it as she made plans with her other friends to meet at this place Hucker's. Amelia was looking forward to meeting other people. Being new in Houston, she wanted to make some friends and get to know the area. With Regan's outgoing personality, Amelia should make some new friends in no time.

Chapter 3

The music was blasting and Amelia was laughing at something Regan's friend Georgia was saying. Amelia was impressed with all the excitement going on around her and the other seven women. Since they walked in an hour ago, they all were approached by some of the sexiest men Amelia had ever seen.

"I told you that you'd love a traditional honky-tonk. Hucker's is one of the best places this side of Houston," Amelia stated loudly to her, even though she was close. Galen approached, wrapping his arms around Regan from behind, making her gasp. She gave him a slap to his arm then the good-looking cowboy kissed her hard on the mouth as Regan reached back and cupped the back of Galen's head.

Amelia felt her own cheeks warm and an appreciation for the scene come over her.

She turned away a second and spotted the large group of guys enjoying the birthday party. She knew that Murphy and his brothers were over there. They hadn't come over this way and now wouldn't be a good time with Regan sucking face with Galen.

"So, this is your Yankee friend?" Galen asked. His deep, thick accent alerted Amelia that he was addressing her.

"Cut that out, Galen. She's my best friend, so stop teasing her," Regan stated. As Amelia looked up at Galen, she caught him looking her body over.

Amelia was on guard. She raised her eyes at him and gave him the once-over back but as if she were unimpressed.

"Sassy, are you? You better watch that, girl. Been some fellas talking 'bout coming on over here and getting to know you."

Amelia felt her belly quiver. She had been dodging offers to dance and teach her to do the two-step since they'd arrived.

She reached over to the bar to take her drink when she felt someone bump into her. Her drink fell over as she stepped out of the way before looking up at some tall guy. He gave her a wink and she could tell he was feeling pretty good. His eyes were glazed over and he swayed as he moved closer.

"Who's your friend, Regan?" he asked and Amelia looked to Regan and Galen.

"Smooth move," Galen said to the guy. Galen shook his head as if he didn't like the guy, and then Regan placed a hand on Amelia's arm and pulled her closer.

"No one who wants to meet you, Buckey."

At the same time Galen's friends came over, and Galen turned to talk to them. Amelia was walking away, along with Regan, when she felt the hand on her arm.

"I want to know your name, baby." She stared up at him.

"Let go of her arm." The voice came from behind her and in a flash, she was surrounded by three extra big men and Murphy.

She could hear Regan saying something, but she couldn't see a thing as these men flanked her, placing her behind them.

"Just being friendly, Mad Dog. No need to come over here with your brothers. This ain't none of your business," she heard Buckey say.

"You okay?" She looked to her right and smack into a black shirt. Tilting her head slowly upward, she finally saw the face of the man who asked her if she was okay.

She nodded her head. He looked mean, pissed off, cold as ice, yet his thick build and big muscles made every feminine instinct react.

When she felt the hand grab her hand, she turned toward Regan. "Buckey won't bother you with my brothers around. Brody, meet Amelia," Regan said and Brody, the one Amelia knew was called Ice, and for obvious reasons, widened his eyes as if surprised by her name.

She reached out to shake his hand and when their fingers met, she felt a shock of awareness and looked back up into his eyes. Something changed in the deep tone of them. They were dark blue, but almost too dark.

She pulled away and looked back at Regan.

Regan smiled then grabbed her arm and pulled her close.

"I told you that my brothers are big men."

"Big? Holy crap," Amelia whispered. Then she heard someone clear his throat and there was a friend of Galen's.

"I'm Michael. Galen told me you were looking for a dance partner. Care to dance?"

"Hi, Michael. Sorry, but I'm not quite ready to venture onto the dance floor and do the two-step. It's been years," she said to the good-looking cowboy. He seemed sweet and completely opposite to the two Haas brothers. Remnants of their dark good looks still lingered in her mind. Michael was not dark, mysterious, or what her body felt as lethal. He was cute. Blond hair, a dimple in his chin, and light green eyes. Why she was comparing, she didn't know, but she did acknowledge the fact that there wasn't an instant spark with Michael like there had been with Murphy and Brody.

"We can go out there together," Regan suggested. She looked up behind Amelia, but before Amelia could turn to see what the exchange was about, Regan smiled.

"Michael, you take it easy on her. Amelia's out of practice."

Michael took Amelia's hand and smiled down at her. "No worries, darling, slow and easy. The way I like it." He placed a hand on her waist and ushered her toward the large crowded dance floor.

She felt the blush hit her cheeks and realized that cowboys sure knew how to flirt and use their Texas accents. Now hopefully, she wouldn't fall flat on her face and make a complete ass out of herself. This Yankee was going to show them that she could do the two-step like a pro.

A quick glance over her shoulder and she saw the four men staring at her. She nearly tripped on the small step that brought them up to the dance floor but Michael grabbed her tight.

"Don't be nervous, sweetheart, I'm right here with you." He turned her backward and off they went. She looked up, uncertain why her eyes zeroed in on the Haas brothers one more time. Mad Dog and Ice looked lethal, and the other two, whom she hadn't met, were just as fierce looking. One had his Stetson real low and he kind of looked familiar. It was hard to see. As Michael began showing her the two-step, she caught sight of the men again. Her heart nearly stopped as she realized that the one brother with bruises on his cheek and near his eye was the same guy from the airport. She swallowed hard as Michael pulled her closer.

* * * *

"That's Amelia?" Ricky asked then took a slug of beer and watched her just like his brothers were. He heard Sniper whistle.

"Wow," he said, staring at the woman. His brother appeared as if he knew what she looked like or something, but Brody knew Sniper had never met Amelia.

"Tell me about it. The first time I met her today, she was wearing a bikini," Mad Dog stated, and his three brothers looked at him. Ricky felt his insides clench up. He didn't know why.

"You met her today?" Ricky asked.

Mad Dog didn't take his eyes off the dance floor or Amelia. A quick glance in that direction and Ricky could see Michael trying to help Amelia do the two-step. His hand was on her lower back, way lower than it had to be.

They didn't say another word, but as Ricky looked at his brothers, their expressions grew darker and they seemed pissed off.

"So it looks like Regan and Galen are an item," Ricky said to his brothers. They made some annoyed sounds.

"I don't like it," Sniper stated.

"I don't like it either, Waylon, but she's a grown woman and she can date whomever she wants to. I tried speaking to her when I stopped by her condo," Mad Dog said.

"That's when you saw Amelia in a bikini?" Ricky couldn't help but ask.

"It wasn't a sight to forget, Scar." Mad Dog looked back at the dance floor.

Ricky looked, too, and now another cowboy was stepping in to dance with Amelia.

"She seems to know the two-step just fine," Brody said in an annoyed voice, and then they were silent.

* * * *

Amelia was getting tired. She had been out here dancing in this circle and dodging roaming hands and flirtatious comments. As the one cowboy, Tucker, spun her around then pressed his chest hard against her, plastering his hand over her ass, she grew annoyed.

She didn't want to make a scene considering that she seemed to have drawn quite the amount of attention from curious onlookers.

"I think I've had it, Tucker. I need a break." She tried to pry his hands from their locked position behind her back.

"Darlin', we're just getting started. I waited a good twenty minutes to get my shot dancing with you."

She didn't care for his tone one bit. The other cowboys she'd danced with were very friendly and respectful. None of them acted like Tucker.

"I suggest you release me right now." Her New York accent came on real thick as he stared down at her. He was built. Just like most of the men she'd danced with. But there was something creepy about his expression.

"Why don't we head outta here, and go somewhere more private, doll."

His statement wasn't a question at all. He basically was telling her that was his plan, but she wasn't interested.

She didn't want to cause a scene or become overly concerned with Tucker's behavior, but as he practically dragged her off the dance floor, she knew she needed to stop him.

She spotted the tray of beer as the waitress stood by the dance floor on the bar side.

"Wait, I said I needed a drink."

Tucker paused as he looked down at her cleavage. "You stalling?"

"I'm not going with you. I don't know you and to be honest, I don't like your attitude."

He pulled her hard against him. "You're coming with me and we're going to continue this party." He pressed her hard against the bar and she gasped at his move.

She looked up at Tucker, recognizing the anger in his eyes, and then she saw Mad Dog standing behind Tucker. The man towered over Tucker. Her eyes probably looked like saucers as Mad Dog tapped on Tucker's shoulder and Tucker turned.

"I don't think the lady wants to leave with you."

"It's none of your business, Murphy. The little lady and me were getting associated on the dance floor. Now she's leaving with me."

"No, I'm not."

Mad Dog gave her a mean-looking expression.

Tucker turned and looked her over. "You're my piece of ass tonight. If Murphy's interested, he can have my seconds."

"What?" she exclaimed, insulted and so damn angry she let her temper flare. She looked around her and to the guys standing next to her. Pulling a beer from one of their hands she took one of the mugs of beer and threw the contents into Tucker's face, also hitting Mad Dog in the process.

Then she stomped forward and pointed her finger in Tucker's chest.

"You listen here, cowboy Casanova, I'm not interested in leaving here with you or any other cowboy. The nerve of you to think that you could actually come up in my face and say the things you're saying and order me to just go along with you." She gave him the once-over then turned around to walk away until he grabbed a hold of her. That was when things turned ugly.

* * * *

Murphy was fuming. He hesitated knocking Tucker's lights out for what he'd said to Amelia, but then she told Tucker off, threw a whole beer at Tucker, hitting Murphy in the process. Now he was really pissed. Because he hesitated, shocked at the guts or maybe stupidity the little woman had as she stuck her finger into Tucker's chest and yelled at him. But the moment Tucker grabbed Amelia from behind, he lost the ability to take things easy.

Gripping Tucker by the back of his shirt collar as Amelia screamed, Tucker came flying backward.

Tucker took a swing at Murphy, but Murphy ducked and took one shot straight to Tucker's nose, knocking him onto the ground. He looked up to see the shocked expression on Amelia's face, then what looked like fear before she turned to take off.

Instead, she ran smack into Ricky.

* * * *

"Are you okay, honey? He didn't hurt you did he?" Ricky asked as Amelia stared up into his eyes looking like a doe caught in headlights.

He caressed her arms, loving the feel of her softness as he inhaled her heavenly scent. Damn did the woman smell edible.

"I'm Regan's brother, Ricky. Come on, let's go sit down."

"What's going on? Did that asshole try something, Amelia?" Regan asked.

Amelia nodded her head.

"I think your brother Murphy is pissed. I kind of threw beer at him," Amelia said and Regan chuckled.

"It was a good shot and mostly landed in Tucker's face," Ricky offered, placing his arm over her shoulder and leading her and Regan toward the bar.

She sidestepped, causing him to move his arm. The woman had a bit of a chip on her shoulder for such a petite little thing. A second glance revealed what appeared like fear. Was she afraid of him? That thought didn't sit right with Ricky. He knew he was a big man and had a hard look about him, just like his brothers. War did that to men and women. He decided to ignore that nagging thought that she was scared of him.

As they arrived, Ricky introduced her to their friends and to Sniper.

"This is Waylon."

Ricky watched Amelia look at the bruises on Waylon's face then turn away from him and toward Regan. Then she looked back at Sniper.

* * * *

"The guy from the airport," she whispered.

Waylon gave her a look that made her thighs quiver, and her pussy stand up at attention. *Oh God, why do these men have to be Regan's brothers? Why this one from the airport?*

He reached his hand out to shake hers.

"Nice to meet you officially, Amelia."

Their hands touched, and Lord have mercy, did she feel the attraction. Regan's brothers were lethal.

He stepped closer and she had to tilt her head all the way back to maintain eye contact with the hunk of a man. Despite the bruises and her inner conscience telling her to run for the hills, she licked her lower lip in appreciation for the man. His eyes zeroed in on her mouth, and then he spoke.

"Seems you nearly got yourself into a situation, darling. You like living on the wild side?" he asked with that damn sexy Texas twang that was making her feel like some stupid bimbo with only sex and lustful thoughts ruling her mind. If she released a sigh right now, that would be the icing on the cake.

She sensed Regan behind her, then felt her hand on her shoulder.

Regan whispered to her. "This is the guy from the airport?"

Amelia rolled her eyes as embarrassment hit her. She'd carried on about the hunk of a man from the airport last night and how she considered him her first introduction to the type of men in Houston. Now she felt embarrassed. This was Regan's brother.

After glancing over her shoulder and stepping away from Waylon, Regan looked like the cat that swallowed the canary. Her shit-eating grin warned Amelia that ideas were swarming around in Regan's head.

"You were right, Regan, some cowboys can be such idiots," Amelia said then shook her head in frustration.

* * * *

Ricky absorbed her petite frame and long black hair. The woman stood out like a goddess. Her skin was tan and her body had curves in all the right places. His brothers noticed, too. Sniper was in a dead stare at her right now. So his brother met Amelia at the airport? Coincidence? Or was it more?

"Maybe you shouldn't have been accepting all those dances with men you don't know," Sniper stated, and Ricky looked toward a shocked Amelia. Regan placed her hands on her hips.

"This wasn't Amelia's fault, Sniper. Tucker is an asshole and you know it."

Sniper looked at Regan and gave her the once-over.

"Should be more careful accepting invitations and letting men you don't know feel you up on the dance floor." Sniper took a slug of beer. Amelia and Regan were shocked. Ricky stood by Sniper and looked at Amelia.

"Or how about refusing help from strangers in airports?" she replied sarcastically.

"He's right. You should watch who you flirt with."

"What? Are you kidding me?" Amelia began to say when Regan stopped her.

"Forget it, Amelia. My brothers are idiots sometimes, too. Just ignore them." Regan grabbed Amelia's arm and they walked away but not before sexy, little Amelia gave Ricky and Sniper a dirty look.

"She. Is. Gorgeous," Ricky whispered, taking a seat next to his brother before swallowing a slug of beer.

"Mad Dog okay?" Sniper asked, never taking his eyes off of Amelia. She and Regan met up with other friends and started talking.

"What do you think?"

"I think it's time to call it a night."

Ricky watched as their friend Captain and a few guys approached Amelia and Regan. Their sister started laughing and Amelia shyly looked away. Ricky wondered what kind of woman she really was. Considering that she was Regan's best friend in college, Regan didn't share too much about Amelia or her family. Ricky didn't even know if she had a family. Then he wondered why he even cared. It wasn't like he was interested in getting to know her better. Ricky looked up to where Amelia stood talking. The longer he watched, the more he realized that she interested him.

He gave Sniper a nudge in the arm when he noticed Sniper watching Amelia, too.

"She's a good-looking woman. Hard to not watch her."

"She's got an attitude that can get her in trouble. She was lucky Mad Dog was there to help her."

"I think we should keep an eye on her whenever we can. She's Regan's friend and she's new around here."

Sniper turned toward Ricky and Ricky kept a straight face. He basically was saying that he was interested in getting to know Amelia better and hoping that Sniper was, too.

"Good luck with that." Sniper placed his empty beer bottle down on the bar then walked away. Ricky watched him as he shook hands with his brothers and some of their friends. That was Sniper. Always keeping his distance, his emotions and feelings hidden. But, he didn't hide his interest in Amelia from Ricky. Ricky never saw his brothers react to any woman, never mind to the same woman.

Looking back to where Amelia stood, he caught her watching Sniper, and then her eyes landed on Ricky's. Ricky winked but kept his expression firm. If there was a chance that he could get close to Amelia, she would learn fast that he was a boss and expected to be in control. He wouldn't be manipulated with jealousy and games. It was why he remained single even now. He hadn't met a sincere woman yet that he was attracted to. But as he watched her and absorbed her sexy, curvy body and sweet smile, he wondered if she were just playing games. He was too old for games.

Chapter 4

"God, Regan, it's so beautiful here. It's amazing," Amelia said as they sat on a swinging bench that looked out over the swimming hole. She could hear the birds singing and felt the gentle caress of the breeze against her shoulders. The bright June sun warmed her skin.

"How do you stay living in the city and not remain out here all the time?"

"And commute? Are you insane? I like being on my own and having my privacy."

Amelia looked at Regan. Her best friend was beautiful. She had golden blonde hair that cascaded over her shoulders, big bright blue eyes, and a dimple in her left cheek. She was very attractive and fun, carefree, but also typical country girl. Aside from her desire to act like she was worldly and ready for action, Regan was a kind soul, and cautious.

Amelia gave her a little bump with her shoulder. "I guess it's tough having brothers around to know your every move."

"Oh God, you have no idea."

Amelia took a deep breath and stared out across the water. She could see the two cowboys slowly riding toward the swimming hole and then watched as the horses lowered their heads toward the water to take a drink. They looked so big and the horses looked small. Not that Amelia knew much about horses, but it appeared as if the cowboys riding them were extra large. She couldn't help but wonder if one of them were one of Regan's brothers. Any of them would be great to see.

"They make me crazy sometimes. Plus my brothers are especially hard and critical. They're ex-military you know. Special Forces, Green Berets, and stuff. Each of them is their own arsenal." Regan gave a small laugh. When Amelia turned to look at her, Regan was raising each of her eyebrows in a silly manner as if hinting at Amelia's obvious attraction to them.

Amelia gave Regan a little shove.

"Cut it out. I'm not interested and they're your brothers. I wouldn't want to cause another fight around them. God knows how Mad Dog or even Sniper, would react," Amelia said sarcastically.

Regan laughed. "They each are a force to reckon with. That's brothers, I guess," Regan said then smiled.

"I wouldn't know. Even when my brothers were alive, life was hard and they were indifferent. You're lucky, you know? To have four brothers who care, and of course three dads, and a mom. God, I can't even get over that still. It's so cool." Amelia leaned back and watched the cowboys. As soon as the horses had their fill, the cowboys headed up toward the area where Amelia and Regan sat. It would take them some time to get up the hill at their slow pace.

"You saw them last night. They were there the moment you needed assistance."

"Murphy did help me out with Tucker. Of course afterward the others did reprimand me. I think Sniper basically said I was immature and flaunted myself, asking for Tucker's actions."

Regan made a sound with her mouth.

"I wouldn't worry about Sniper. He keeps to himself and mostly has nothing nice to say anyway. My brothers can be indifferent, too. I think being in the military hardened them and made them untrusting."

"Your brothers were in the military for a long time. Of course they're affected. But they seem pretty confident and they're all working."

"I guess so. I mean it is obvious that they care. It just gets on my nerves sometimes. I think the best part of last night, was finally meeting your mystery airport man, that ultimately introduced you to the sexy possibilities of living the single life in Houston." Regan teased Amelia. Amelia felt her cheeks warm as she shook her head.

"Yeah, well first impressions are kind of screwed up and inaccurate sometimes."

Regan laughed.

"I'm going to head up to check my cell phone, and to see if Galen called. My sister, Velma, asked me to check out the three outfits she brought for her birthday in two weeks."

Regan stood up and smiled.

"She's beautiful and looks way older than twenty. I bet your brothers will start worrying about her and maybe give you some slack." Amelia winked. Regan chuckled.

"Honey, you don't know the Haas brothers like I do. Will you be okay out here by yourself?"

"I'm going to sit just for a little while longer. I promised your mom that I would help her with dinner."

"She'll love that, just as I'm sure that everyone will love that cheesecake you made."

Amelia smiled then leaned back and closed her eyes. She started thinking about her new life here. The hospital was ten minutes from the condo and Regan said she spoke to Murphy about finding an apartment to rent near her new job. Of course Regan said she was fine with having Amelia stay with her for however long, but Amelia overheard Galen asking about sleeping over, and Regan denied him. Amelia didn't want to stand in the way of her friend's love life.

She crossed her legs and allowed the relaxing atmosphere to ease her mind.

She wasn't too surprised that she thought of her brothers, Kyle and Edward. She really thought that she could have saved Kyle. But she learned that people have to have some bit of hope of desire to live, or else it was useless. Why couldn't she have brothers like Regan did? As the thought hit her mind, she realized that she wouldn't want them as brothers. She couldn't even pretend to see them in that light or with that label. Seeing them as brothers was the farthest thing from her mind.

"How did you find one of the best spots on the ranch?"

Amelia jumped as she sat forward and looked behind her. The sudden sound of a man's voice startled her.

"Oh God, Ricky, you scared me."

She watched as Ricky walked around the bench and stared down at her. He kept one hand on his hip and holster. It was taking some getting used to, seeing so many people carrying firearms wherever they went. Back in New York, weapons were concealed, and usually carried by cops and thugs. Ricky was sporting a black gun. She had no clue what kind because he looked so sexy.

"Didn't mean to scare you, darling. You looked so lost in thought," he said and she tried to look into his eyes, but the black Stetson he wore was low. It made him appear dangerous. She had the silly "butterflies in her stomach" sensation, and she wasn't certain why.

"It's so peaceful out here. You all must have loved growing up on the ranch," she said as she pried her eyes off of the man and forced herself to look toward the two men getting down off the horses. *Mad Dog.*

She didn't know who the other guy was. Her eyes zeroed in on Mad Dog and how his presence instantly magnified the atmosphere around them.

"It was the best way to grow up. Living off the land, working on the farm and in the fields. It's very beautiful," Ricky said as he held her gaze then lowered himself to the seat next to her.

She adjusted her position as his thick, hard thigh made contact with her bare one. Perhaps wearing pants would have been the better option today.

"Howdy."

She looked up as Mad Dog and another young cowboy tipped their hats at her.

"Hi," she replied.

"I'm Jonas. You must be Amelia, Regan's friend."

He reached his hand out and she accepted it as he held her gaze. This cowboy was much younger than Mad Dog and Ricky. His green eyes sparkled as he looked her thighs over.

"Nice to meet you, Jonas."

"So what are you doing out here all alone?" Mad Dog asked and he sounded kind of pissed.

She looked over her shoulder toward the house, way in the distance, and her belly tightened from his reprimanding tone.

"Regan just headed inside. I was enjoying the quietness." Damn her shaky voice. Mad Dog Murphy was such a disciplinary man.

Mad Dog stared down at her. His dark blue eyes sparkled as his eyes roamed over her body. There was no denying it. Mad Dog and Ricky affected her. So she focused on Jonas.

"So, where are you staying? Has Regan given you a tour of town and some of the hot spots?" Jonas asked as he stood next to her. She decided to stand up, feeling the heat of Ricky's thigh next to hers. As she stood, a light breeze collided against her skin, sending her long, black hair over her shoulders. Her skirt lifted slightly because of the flared bottom edge and she grabbed onto it to keep it in place. In doing so, she nearly lost her balance, her legs so shaky from having Mad Dog staring at her, watching her every move, and Ricky doing the same thing.

"Whoa," Jonas said as he reached for her and steadied her by her waist.

"I'm okay. Thank you," she said to Jonas who smiled down at her then released his hold and tipped his hat. "No problem, ma'am."

"Jonas, want to take the horses back to the stable for us. We'll call it a day. We should walk Amelia back up to the house," Mad Dog stated firmly, surprising Jonas but also making Amelia jump from his commanding tone.

"It was nice meeting you, Amelia. I'm sure I'll see you around."

"Yes, nice meeting you, too," she replied then thought she heard a noise behind her.

Jonas took the reins of both horses and walked them over toward a large stable. She watched him go, thinking that Jonas was very nice and that the horses were gorgeous creatures.

"Didn't you learn last night about flirting?"

She turned toward Ricky and was a bit taken aback by his comment.

"What are you talking about?" Ricky looked her over and she had to turn away from his gaze that totally affected her. She wound up looking straight up into Mad Dog's eyes and he didn't look happy. His arms were crossed in front of his chest as he watched her.

"Last night, after you were dancing with every cowboy in the place and Tucker decided you wanted him to take you home," Ricky stated.

She was so annoyed. The anger hit her insides as she gave him a dirty look.

"First of all, I was not flirting and nor did I dance with every cowboy in the place. Secondly, Ricky, it's none of your business." He took a step toward her and instantly she reacted, taking numerous steps back. She knew that look, or at least she thought she did. Men hit women all the time or manhandled them. These men were soldiers and they were cowboys. Two things she was completely staying away from.

"Maybe I'm making it my business. Regan's been acting a bit wild lately. She should have warned you about Hucker's and the types of cowboys that hang out there," Ricky said.

"You were there," she retorted, mostly just to zing him. He was making her feel very nervous. Ricky was almost as big as Mad Dog, had just as many muscles, and ultimately was just so damn good looking, she felt faintish. Never in her life had a man, or more than one man, made her feel this way.

Ricky gently took her hand into his large ones, and began to caress his fingers over her palm. She felt that tingling sensation go from her hand, straight to her pussy from his touch. Hot damn, did this man know how to be suave? She wasn't born yesterday. Then for a moment she wondered if he were just being considerate because she was Regan's friend.

"We had a party to go to. Listen, I'm just telling you to watch yourself. You're a petite little thang, and any man could try to have his way with you, especially if you're sending out the wrong signals." *Maybe not so suave after all.*

"For crying out loud. Are you for real? I don't remember asking you for advice or asking for you to keep an eye on me. You know what, I don't want to get into an argument with my best friend's brothers. Why don't you just mind your business and I'll mind mine." She turned around hoping her words halted them from any other communication. These two men made her shake.

"Amelia."

She stopped then looked over her shoulder toward Mad Dog. She wasn't sure why. Maybe it was his deep tone, the Texas accent, or simply the man's ability to make anyone halt in their tracks with just one word.

"We'll talk later."

She turned back around and headed toward the house. Who the heck was Mad Dog to say "we'll talk later"? Was he for real? God, Regan's brothers sure did take the protective role seriously. But why include her? She wasn't even family.

As she got closer to the house, she saw Regan standing on the front porch with Velma.

"Were they bothering you?" Regan asked.

"Apparently, I'm a flirt who sends guys the wrong messages. I don't know." Amelia threw her arms up in the air.

Regan chuckled then winked at Velma.

"My brothers have the hots for you," Velma said and Amelia gasped.

"What? No, not me. They're all acting like I'm their sister, too. Regan, you can keep them. I don't need this type of aggravation."

Regan and Velma laughed.

"I have to see this play out. This is awesome," Velma said and Amelia didn't know what the little Haas woman meant, but all she wanted to do was stay clear of Mad Dog and Ricky.

* * * *

"So, you start on Monday right, Amelia?" Elise Haas asked as Amelia, Regan, and Velma set the large table. It could seat more than a dozen people, and as Amelia thought about that, she realized there were going to be eleven of them eating today. Her belly tightened at the thought that all four Haas brothers were going to be sitting there.

"Amelia?"

"Oh, sorry, Mrs. Haas. I was just thinking about how huge this table is."

Elise smiled.

"Wait until you see this place in two weeks, Amelia. The whole family is going to be here and a bunch of friends for my birthday," Velma stated with a smile as she placed the napkins next to each place setting.

"That's right, you're turning twenty-one. Very cool," Amelia added.

"So what about the job, Amelia?" Elise asked as her husbands, Sam, Jordan, and Tysen, entered the room. They each gave their wife a kiss or a pat to her backside. She swatted their hands away and giggled. Amelia smiled. It was nice to see the affection and love between the four of them and it was weird, too.

"Well, I'm a bit nervous, obviously," she began to say then noticed Ricky and Brody standing in the doorway. Their brothers Waylon and Murphy were already taking a seat at the table.

She swallowed hard. They saw her watching their fathers and mother. But who couldn't get caught in appreciating their obvious love.

"Well that's understandable, Amelia. Starting a new job can be nerve-racking, but I'm sure you'll do just fine. I heard that your interview knocked their socks off," Sam Haas stated then popped a cherry tomato into his mouth.

"How did you hear about my interview?"

"Oh, I know your boss, Toby Conlin."

"Oh."

"Where is she working, the hospital?" Ricky asked, sounding annoyed and she wondered why.

"She's working in the injured soldier program. Amelia has a big heart." Regan winked as she locked gazes with Amelia. Amelia shook her head. Regan was enjoying using Amelia to egg her brothers on.

"Why do you ask, Ricky?"

"Well, last night Tucker tried to take Amelia home with him," he stated with his arms crossed in front of his chest. Now all four brothers stared at her. Amelia felt her cheeks warm and then she heard Sam, Jordan, and Tysen make comments.

"That man is trouble. I hope you four did something about it," Jordan stated.

"She's standing here now isn't she?" Mad Dog replied with an attitude.

Amelia wanted the floor to eat her up. This was so embarrassing. Where did all this instant protectiveness come from? She wasn't used to it. She took care of herself and the sooner everyone understood that the better.

"Excuse me," she stated. They all looked at her as Elise, Regan, and Velma placed the last platters of food onto the table.

"I don't know anything about Tucker or what his problem was last night. I don't know any of you at all really. I appreciate your concern. I appreciated your assistance last night, Murphy, but I'm a big girl and I can take care of myself. I've been doing it long enough, so please, back off."

By the intense expressions on the men's faces, she knew she hit a sore spot or something with them. She heard chuckling as she turned toward their fathers. She saw them trying not to laugh.

Elise smiled as she patted Amelia's shoulder.

"You have been taking care of yourself, Amelia. But my boys will keep an eye on you, for me. You're not from around here. You don't know who to stay clear of and what things to watch out for. And don't worry, my sons' barks are bigger than their bites. So let's eat, before it gets cold."

Jordan pulled a chair out for Amelia as Sam pulled one out for his wife. She sat between her men, and they served her first before they served themselves.

Feeling half successful in making a stand and half foolish, they ate in silence until Velma began to explain about her plans for next Friday night, her official birthday, and then the family party here at the house on Sunday.

Amelia caught the looks from the Haas brothers. She felt her palms sweating as their intimidating personas affected her big-time.

She took a piece of chicken and looked up to find Sniper watching her. She liked both of his names. Waylon sounded so cowboyish. Sniper definitely added to his intimidating attitude. The way his eyes held her gaze, or zeroed in on her body, her lips especially as she spoke, made her nervous and aroused. A glance at each of them, and she saw things she liked and was attracted to and things she feared. The ultimate scare was their immediate authoritative attitude. They were bossy, mean looking, yet handsome enough to stop a woman dead in her tracks. She smiled to herself. *Son of a bitch, I am attracted to these men. Since I would never be able to choose between them if I had a chance, it's futile to fantasize.*

"Waylon, you'll be here for my birthday right? You don't have any matches?" Velma asked.

Amelia wondered what Velma was talking about, and as she looked at Waylon, he gave a nice smile to his sister.

"No boxing matches. I'll be here."

Amelia's stomach was immediately in knots.

"You're a boxer, a fighter?" she asked, her voice cracking as she said the words.

"Yeah, that's where his bruises came from. He just finished a huge match in Vegas. That's when you guys first met right? At the airport." Regan smiled, but Amelia wasn't even paying so much attention to that or how his parents began asking about them meeting. She heard them saying how crazy it was that she and Waylon met one another at the airport. She even heard Velma say something about fate, but Amelia was in a dead stare at Waylon and she felt the disappointment and sadness reach her eyes.

He's a fighter. He has a bad attitude. He's just like what I left back in New York.

"You should see him fight. He's really good, Amelia," Velma stated.

She stared at her plate.

"I don't like fighting," she whispered.

"Oh this is organized fighting. You should see how good Waylon is," Regan added.

Amelia was silent. She felt the eyes upon her and then Jordan changed the subject and they all started talking about the ranch, the upcoming season, and swimming in the lake out back.

She listened quietly as they all talked about the area.

"Murphy, did you get a chance to look for a place for Amelia to rent yet? Didn't you say he was going to help her, Regan?" Elise asked.

"Yeah, Murphy, anything?" Regan asked.

Murphy looked at his mom as he wiped the corner of his mouth with a blue checkered linen napkin.

"I've been looking. I found a few places, but the rent isn't cheap."

"How much?" Amelia asked.

He looked at Amelia from directly across the table.

"A few hundred more than what Regan said you could afford."

"Shoot. Well, don't worry, Amelia, you can stay with me for however long you need to," Regan said.

"I don't want to impose like that. I'll look around, too. I'm just a bit wary of taking on too high of a rent before I even get my first few paychecks. Once I sign a lease, I'm stuck. What if the job doesn't work out, or if I need the money for something else? I'm already using public transportation until my car gets here from New York."

"It will get here this week right?" Regan asked.

"It's supposed to."

"I have a great idea. Especially since the hospital is only about thirty minutes from here. Why not stay in the bunkhouse down the road? It's completely renovated. No one is renting it right now," Elise stated.

"Oh, Mom, that's a great idea," Regan said with a smile. Amelia didn't know what to say.

"Oh, I don't know, Mrs. Haas. I mean, I don't have a car as is and Monday I start work."

"You can take your time moving in once you get settled with your job and your car arrives. You don't have to pay us rent until you're settled," Sam added.

"Yeah, the men and I will make sure it's all set up for you, the grass mowed, and everything working correctly," Jordan said then looked at his sons. They all looked a bit pissed off except for Ricky. Ricky had a sly little smirk on his face.

"I'll pay the rent. Whatever it is, if you're sure that you don't mind having me here?"

"Are you kidding? It's a great idea. I wish I had thought of it," Regan said and smiled.

Amelia wasn't too sure, but as she thought about Regan and her friend's love life, she accepted Elise's offer.

"Thank you so much, Mrs. Haas. Mr. Mr. and Mr. Haas," Amelia said then chuckled. They all laughed.

"Just call us by our first names, honey. You're family now," Elise stated and Amelia felt the tears reach her eyes.

If only that were true.

Chapter 5

"So how were your first two weeks of working here, Amelia? Feeling comfortable yet?" her new boss, Toby Conlin, asked.

She was a bit overwhelmed with the caseload and trying to organize the group activities for the next week.

"It's a lot of work, but I think I'll come up with a system in no time."

He smiled at her as he leaned against her desk. He was an attractive man. Older, in his fifties and divorced. He had a girlfriend, Mary, whom Amelia met just yesterday afternoon.

"So, what do you think of the group members and the numerous groups we offer for the veterans?"

Amelia swallowed that uneasy feeling in her gut. It was more difficult than she expected. These groups had a lot of men who were maimed or severely injured in the war.

"Honestly, it was a bit tough at first. There are so many emotions going on in the groups. But I'm impressed with the numbers. Back in New York, there were very small groups. A lot of men refused help, even those who got into trouble with abusing alcohol or drugs." As she said the words, her heart ached for them and for the memories of her brothers and father.

"We talked about this yesterday. The way you assisted Carter was amazing. He's had difficulty opening up and accepting help."

"I could tell that he wanted to talk. I knew something was up with him immediately. I just don't know what made him take those pills. You said he's been coming here for the last three months."

"It happens, Amelia. Sometimes even the consistent attendees fall back to bad habits. But you have great ideas to keep them motivated to continue. I especially like your idea about some trips out of the hospital. A lot of these men don't have any family."

"I know. I guess I can empathize with them in that category." She pulled together her things, preparing to leave for the weekend.

"You have the Haas family. They speak very highly of you. It's almost like you're their daughter." He stood straight and watched her gather her things.

She felt the blush hit her cheeks. "I'm not though. They're just really nice."

"They adopted Brody and Waylon when they were just kids. Their mother died and their father disappeared on them. He was a lowlife from the start."

"Really? I mean, I knew that they were adopted, but not the story behind it."

"Well, Elise, Sam, Jordan, and Tysen share something very special. They have huge hearts and would do anything to help someone in need."

"I know. Regan and Velma are lucky to have them."

They heard a knock on the door and Felicia was there.

"Hi, Felicia," Toby said and motioned for her to come in. Amelia said hello, too.

"I'm so glad I caught you two before you leave. I have a situation for Saturday morning."

"What's going on?"

"Well, Ryan called. He can't run the table from eight until twelve. I don't have a replacement."

"Well, what does it entail?" Amelia asked.

"You get to sweat your butt off for four hours, smile, flirt, do whatever, to sell raffle tickets to our July fundraiser event. This year, we're having a family day picnic on Sonoma Lake. We'd like to pay for everything ourselves, so that the soldiers and their families can just enjoy themselves. A lot of them are on fixed incomes or barely making it."

"Well, I would love to help. I was only planning on moving into the cottage, but I can do that in the afternoon. I'm behind schedule, since my car arrived from New York so late. But I don't have much to move," Amelia volunteered.

"Oh God, Amelia, are you sure?" Felicia asked.

"Yes. Definitely. Just give me directions to where I have to be and whom I have to report to and I'll be there tomorrow morning."

Felicia hugged Amelia and Amelia was shocked.

"I knew you were an angel. I just knew it. Just a few minutes in a room with you, and it's obvious how loving and compassionate you are. Thank you. I'll write everything down for you now," Felicia said then walked out of the room to get paper and a pen.

Amelia looked at Toby and he smiled.

"She's right, you know? You're an asset to the program and the guys. The families are saying positive things about you. Your personal insight into their emotions is compelling."

She felt embarrassed a moment as she lowered her eyes.

"I guess I just understand what they're going through and want to help them any way I can."

"I'm surprised that your degree isn't in counseling or social work. You would be great."

"I appreciate that. But, I like what I do. I like organizing and planning. When there's a positive end result, then I'm satisfied and feel complete."

Toby smiled. "Well, I guess we'll call it a night. I'll probably see you at the fair tomorrow. I'm helping to run the dunking tank. The guys from the fire department offered half the donation money if I assisted. I think they're going to try to talk me into sitting in the damn thing."

Amelia laughed then tapped him on the shoulder. "It's all for a good cause, boss."

He chuckled as they headed out of the office. Felicia waved good-bye after handing Amelia directions and details on the event.

* * * *

The moment Murphy arrived at eleven o'clock he spotted Amelia. His heart was hammering in his chest and his blood pressure shot nearly to the moon. She was working at a raffle table, currently surrounded by a half a dozen men, and she was laughing. She wore a gorgeous-looking yellow halter dress that accentuated her large breasts, trim waist, and of course her toned, tanned arms. She looked like a goddess. Her hair was braided on some fancy style and bunched around her head in some intricate design. As he moved closer, he noticed the tiny yellow flowers scattered here and there between the braided hair. She looked beautiful.

"You know her?"

Murphy turned toward Big Jay Sandstone, a buddy of his from the service who now served in SWAT. His two brothers, Duke and Sandman, were looking at some artwork with their woman, Grace. They were pushing a stroller with Emma, their firstborn baby girl, and another baby was on the way. Murphy was envious.

"Yeah, she's Regan's friend from college. She's from New York."

Big Jay placed his hand on Murphy's shoulder.

"You look like you're going to start tossing those guys."

Murphy crossed his arms in front of his chest. He was about the same size as Big Jay, and standing together, he knew they totally looked intimidating.

"Why would I do that?"

Big Jay chuckled as he slapped him on the back then proceeded toward the table where Amelia was.

He followed behind and had to hide a chuckle when the cowboys spotted Big Jay then quickly departed.

"Hey, beautiful, what are you selling raffles for?" Big Jay asked. Amelia stared up at Big Jay, eyes wide like saucers. She turned toward Murphy, did a double take, then smoothed out her dress.

"Raising money for the veterans and a family barbeque that's coming up. Would you like to buy some? They're six for five dollars or twelve chances for ten dollars."

"Hmm, I think I'll take ten, honey. Those cowboys weren't bothering you were they?" Big Jay asked.

"No, sir, they were just being friendly."

"You don't have to 'sir' him, doll. This is a friend of mine, Big Jay Sandstone," Murphy stated. As she handed over his tickets and took the ten dollars, Big Jay took her hand and brought it up to his lips. He kissed the top of it as he held her gaze and really pissed Murphy off.

"Cut it out. You're taken," Murphy stated.

"He sure is. What are you two trying to do, scare this poor young woman?"

Murphy turned to see Grace, Duke, and Sandman.

Murphy made the introductions and Amelia stepped around toward the front of the table to see the baby.

"Oh goodness, she is beautiful. How old is she?" Amelia asked.

"Six months and thank you."

Amelia smiled then looked up toward the three big men.

"So, you're Regan's friend from college?" Grace asked after Murphy told the men who she was and how he knew Amelia.

"Yes. I just moved here from New York two weeks ago. I'm working at the veteran's hospital as a program coordinator. They were short staffed today and I volunteered to help out. We're trying to raise money for a family barbeque for the soldiers and their families that are part of the programs we offer."

"That is awesome," Grace said.

"I'll buy some," Sandman stated then passed over a twenty.

"Me, too," Duke said and Murphy laughed.

A few minutes later they were saying good-bye.

"Hey, you should bring Amelia by Casper's sometime. They're having outdoor barbeque parties every Saturday this summer. Tell Regan, too," Big Jay said before he shook Murphy's hand good-bye.

Murphy smiled. His buddies assumed that he was interested in Amelia and that they were already involved. Didn't they know him by now? Murphy didn't date and he didn't trust women. He was such a hard-ass all the time, and most women were turned off.

Amelia began to move past him, and on instinct or maybe just the need to touch her, he grabbed her wrist. She paused next to him and he inhaled the light, floral fragrance of her perfume. It was appealing not pungent.

"You look pretty in this dress."

"Thank you." She moved toward the back of the table.

He watched her as she smoothed out the front of the dress again with her hands. The movement caused her breasts to push together and as she bent slightly, he was able to see the deep cleavage of her breasts. The woman was voluptuous.

"So when are you moving in?" he asked her and she jerked her head up toward him, obviously confused by the statement.

"To the cottage on the ranch. I thought you were doing that today."

"Oh, yes, I am, later on. Like I was telling your friends, this was unexpected, but they needed my help. Plus my car only arrived two days ago. It's been crazy."

"What time do you have to stay until?"

"Noontime. Then Felicia is going to take over until four o'clock."

"I'll help you move so that it won't take too long," Murphy told her as he stood by the table with one hand on his hip. Three guys came up and bought some tickets before she could reply to his statement. They flirted with her and she was polite, but didn't flirt back. Did she do that because he was there? Maybe she was a flirt and a tease?

His mind screamed that he was wrong. She was too sweet.

"Thank you and have a nice day," she told them.

He noticed the folded paper on the table. She didn't even look at it. Instead she tossed it into a box on the ground.

"What was that?"

"Huh?"

"That, you just tossed into the box?"

"Oh, just a phone number."

"A phone number?" He leaned over and looked at the multiple pieces of paper in the box on the floor.

"Guys have been dropping their phone numbers to you on paper?" He raised his voice and she quickly looked around them, then back at him.

"Not a big deal," she replied.

He felt that blood pressure rise again. This woman got under his skin in every aspect of the words.

He looked at his watch.

"You don't have to help me today. I can handle it, Murphy. I know you have a lot to do for Velma's party on Sunday."

"No, I'm good. My brothers and I can handle it. It will be a little bit relaxing tonight."

"Really?" she asked, sounding surprised.

"Why do you say it like that?"

"Well, it's Velma's twenty-first birthday and she's going out partying. I thought for sure you would be acting like bodyguards and escorting her everywhere she went."

"Hey, I've got people watching her. You know, keeping an eye on things."

Amelia held his gaze. "Regan, too?" she teased then ran the palm of her hand across the empty part of the table. Murphy grabbed her hand, covered it, and leaned forward.

"Maybe, I even have people keeping an eye on you."

She looked at his bottom lip. He absorbed the feel of her small, delicate hand beneath his much larger one.

"Why would you do that?"

He licked his bottom lip and saw her eyes watch the motion. "Because, you need watching over. A beautiful woman like you could get herself in a heap of trouble if she weren't careful."

"I don't think so."

He patted her hand.

"Don't you worry. Unless you do something wrong, then I'll find out."

She pulled her hand from his and placed her hands on her hips.

Amelia looked so fucking hot like that. Defiant, sexy, and downright fuckable. His cock was so damn hard right now, he hated to move an inch or he would feel the pain.

"Are you trying to get me all riled up again, Murphy? It's not going to work. You're not the boss of me, remember that," she stated as another group of people, this time a family, came over to buy some tickets. Murphy tipped his Stetson at them and greeted the man.

"How are you doing, Murphy?" Jim Tempo asked. "I haven't seen you around here in months."

"Yeah, been busy helping out the dads on the ranch."

"Running all those businesses your brothers and you are involved in, too. You're doing well. How is Waylon? Last I heard, he had a hell of a fighting match in Vegas. Came back with some bruises, huh? Maybe he'll think of quitting soon. Settling down. That's what all four of you should do."

Murphy raised his eyebrow at Jim. "Have to find the perfect woman. I think you snatched her up before one of the Haas men could," Murphy teased as he winked at Jim's wife.

Betty blushed then shook her head. She turned toward Amelia. "You watch out for this one. He's as stubborn as a mule and then some."

"I'm stubborn? You were the one who stood me up in high school for this guy," Murphy stated as Jim gave his wife a hug and chuckled.

"Sure did." She winked at her husband. They said good-bye and Murphy shook his head. He was still smiling when he turned toward Amelia.

Amelia had her arms crossed in front of her chest, her eyebrows raised in question at his obvious friendly banter with friends. He scowled at her. "What?"

"Nothing," she replied then looked down.

He moved closer, placed his fingers under her chin, and tilted her face up toward him.

She appeared shocked by his move. Well damn, he shocked himself.

"What?" he asked.

"Just surprised to see Mad Dog knows how to smile and not bite."

He stared at her sensual lips. He held her gaze, saw her dark brown eyes sparkling, and wondered what type of lover she would be.

"Maybe I like to bite," he whispered, and she pulled her lower lip between her bottom teeth. He stepped closer. He caressed his thumb along her bottom lip.

"You seem real edible, Miss Amelia. You should watch your sassiness. I don't think you can handle it."

She hesitated then squinted her eyes at him. "I can handle anything you could dish out."

"Excuse me."

Amelia and Murphy turned toward the little boy standing by the table with a ten dollar bill in his hand.

"Yes?" Amelia asked. Reluctantly, Mad Dog immediately released her. This kid had bad timing.

"I would like to donate this ten dollars. I want to help the veterans have a barbeque."

"Aww, that's so sweet. Here are your tickets. Good luck."

"Thank you. Oh, and your boyfriend is huge. Is he a soldier?" the boy asked, and Mad Dog gave the kid a wink.

"Sure am."

"Cool. I want to be a Marine when I'm old enough. My dad and my granddad were Marines." He turned toward his mom who stood alone with two children. Murphy recognized her immediately. She had lost her husband last year. He'd died in Afghanistan.

He gave a wave and the woman waved back.

"Have a nice day," the kid said then walked away.

* * * *

Amelia could see the sadness in Murphy's eyes. His conversation with the little boy gave her that kick in her ass to remind her that she didn't get involved with military men.

Been there. Done that. Got the scars to show for it.

"He was cute. A very respectful kid."

"Yeah, he's a good kid. His mom works two jobs to support them now. I hadn't seen the kid in about a year. He had a rough time when his dad died."

"He died?"

"Yes, in Afghanistan. It was rough for a while."

"I'm sure it was."

"So, it's nearly noontime. Where's this Felicia lady so that I can escort you to your car?"

"Um, Murphy. I don't think it's a good idea."

"If what's a good idea?" a deep, sexy voice asked from behind.

They turned to see Ricky approaching the table.

"Hey, Scar. What's going on?"

"You tell me. Damn, Amelia, you look beautiful in that dress."

"She sure does. I don't think I've ever seen this station so busy all day," Felicia stated as she joined the conversation.

"Thank you so much for helping out on such short notice today, Amelia. You're such an angel."

"It was no problem, Felicia."

Amelia bent down to grab her things.

"This is Murphy and his brother Ricky Haas. Murphy, Ricky, meet Felicia," Amelia said then placed the strap of her purse onto her shoulder.

"Nice to meet you."

"Same here."

When Amelia looked up, Felicia was staring at Murphy and Ricky and then she actually winked. It was obvious that she found both men attractive. Who wouldn't? But for some crazy reason, that upset Amelia.

I'm jealous. Why? I made the decision to not get involved with anyone in the military or anyone who fights or boxes. That covers the Haas brothers. So why are my nipples hard, and why does my belly feel queasy?

"Ready, Amelia? I promised to walk you to your car then help you move today," Murphy said then tipped his hat at Felicia.

Amelia gave the woman a look, and of course she didn't even notice Amelia. She was looking Murphy over.

"I bet you could lift some really heavy boxes with muscles like yours," Felicia stated.

In her mind, Amelia imagined telling Felicia she had something on her lip, then she would whisper the word drool. But she wouldn't. It wasn't her business if the woman was making a complete ass out of herself. Plus, when Amelia looked at Murphy, he seemed to read exactly what was going on. Ricky, however, was his cool suave self. "Pleasure meeting you, Felicia."

"Same here," Felicia responded.

"Bye," Amelia said and as she began walking away, she felt Murphy's hand against her lower back, guiding her through the small crowd.

She directed Murphy toward her car. Ricky came up on her other side.

She was both annoyed and nervous. Annoyed that she felt jealous and nervous because Murphy and Ricky were flanking her on either side and were quite large.

She walked closer to her car, which just happened to be parked under the shade and in the corner of a parking lot behind a large black SUV.

She reached into her purse and pulled the keys out.

"Well thank you for walking me. Perhaps you'd like to go back and mingle a bit?" she said as she unlocked the door. Murphy pulled it open.

"I said I would help you move. Are you headed to Regan's?" Murphy asked in such a hard tone she wondered who the hell he thought he was.

"Yes," she replied, looking up at him.

"Good. We'll follow you," Murphy stated. Ricky winked at her before he reached for the door handle of the SUV parked right beside her car.

Did they park next to her on purpose?

Amelia got behind the wheel and tried starting the engine. It turned over a few times, and just as Ricky opened his door and she cursed her old hunk of junk, it started. She banged her hand on the steering wheel.

"Thank you, God! Please let this car last a few months. Once I save some money, secure this job and the apartment, then I can get something better."

* * * *

"So what do you think?" Ricky asked Murphy as they followed Amelia's car to the condominium complex. He felt nervous and unsure about this. By the expression on Murphy's face, something serious went down in the park today. His brother's hands gripped the steering wheel tight and he could practically see the white of his knuckles.

"Okay, what's the deal? Something go down before I got there?" Ricky asked.

Murphy remained straight faced.

"We should have Brody check over her car. It sounded like the starter was going. What if she's coming home from work late and gets caught all alone on the side of the road? Then what?"

Ricky squinted his eyes at Murphy. His brother was as tough as they came. He was the oldest, the biggest, and Ricky was certain that he never saw Murphy act like this. Whenever Murphy was around Amelia, his Mad Dog personality showed more than anything. It was like he was in military, protective mode. Ricky just wasn't sure about his brother's feelings. Sure, he was attracted to Amelia. Ricky saw the two of them standing close, Murphy towering over her with his fingers holding her chin. Instead of being jealous, Ricky felt aroused, excited, yet, scared.

He and his brothers kept to themselves and didn't date. So why was he thinking about sharing Amelia with them? Why was he hoping to talk her into it? Especially since he was the one with the hang-up about his scars?

He swallowed hard.

"Did you hear me? I think Brody should check her car over for her. Call him. Tell him we'll be there within the hour."

Ricky pulled out his cell. "What was going on between you and Amelia when I showed up along with her friend from work?"

"Nothing. What do you mean?"

"Don't tell me 'nothing.' I saw the way you were staring down at her face, watching her lips, wanting to taste her. You held her chin and she just stood there looking so innocent and beautiful."

Murphy gave his brother a mean expression.

"You don't know what you saw. She challenged me. I challenged her back. It was stupid and it won't happen again."

"Challenged you? How so?"

"Will you stop with the fifty questions? We were just talking. There were all these guys showing up and buying raffle tickets from her. When I got there, there were half a dozen cowboys surrounding her."

Ricky felt his temper rise as he scrunched up his eyebrows and turned toward Murphy.

"Were they bothering her? Did you get rid of them?" Ricky asked.

"Big Jay was with me. We both went over, then Duke, Grace, and Sandman with the baby came over."

Ricky nodded his head. Every time he thought about some other man looking at Amelia, trying to flirt with her, never mind touch her, it filled him with rage. He wanted to hit something. The attraction, the possessiveness came out of nowhere. Like a fucking Mack truck, he was instantly possessive. It seemed that Murphy was feeling the same way.

Murphy pulled up next to Amelia's car as she parked in the parking lot.

* * * *

Amelia noticed Regan's car in the corner and Galen's truck a few spaces down. She prayed that they were in the middle of something as she dialed Regan's cell number. Regan said they were going out. Were she and Galen inside, in bed together? *Oh shit!*

She frantically dialed again as Ricky stood by her door. She put up her finger, indicating for him to hold on a second as she pretended to talk on the phone and the damn thing kept ringing. It was the third time she tried calling and she wished she had Galen's number. Amelia was about to hang up.

"What's wrong?" Regan asked, sounding out of breath.

"If you have your man in there, may I suggest getting dressed, making the bed, and pretending to be cooking something. Your brothers are here to help me move."

"Fuck!"

Amelia heard Regan scream and she couldn't help but laugh.

"Stall them. Oh God, do whatever you have to. Please, Amelia," she begged then disconnected the call.

Amelia felt the instant anxiety slowly release since she got through to Regan, but one look out of her window at a scowling Murphy and she was shaking.

Slowly she got out of the car. She looked around the area and saw a walkway that led to the gardens. It would be obvious that she was stalling if she suggested walking that way.

"Is everything okay?" Ricky asked as he closed her door for her.

"Yes," she whispered, staring up at him and Murphy. They were so tall and handsome, yet they looked hard, almost unemotional. Well not totally unemotional. But the Haas brothers sure had "pissed off" and "untrusting" down pat.

She walked really slow. So much so, that Murphy stopped to stare at her.

"Are you okay? Something hurting?" he asked with concern. She was embarrassed. *Damn, Regan. You knew I would be back by noontime or so.*

She smiled up at him. "I guess I'm a little stiff from standing all morning. Sitting in the car was the only rest I had gotten. I must be out of shape."

Ricky stopped her, took her hands into his, and held her arms out as he looked her body over. "Amelia, you look to be in perfect shape to me." He winked and she blushed. She knew she did. She felt her hot cheeks followed by a wave of heat. Ricky was so good at this.

"I bet you say that to a lot of women. Pretty smooth, Ricky, but I'm not biting." She pulled away and began walking, then reminded herself about moving slowly.

As they entered the front entryway, Amelia saw Will and Paul, the two men who lived there, too. They had talked to her yesterday about hanging out this weekend.

"Hi, Amelia," Paul said then looked up at Murphy and Ricky, almost in shock and disappointment. Paul and Will were really nice guys. They weren't military, boxers, fighters, dominant men, but instead very calm, kind of boring, and worked in business and accounting. They were safe, so she felt comfortable. But she realized, neither man affected her like the Haas brothers.

"Hi, Paul. These are two of Regan's brothers. They're helping me move to the cottage today."

"Hello," he said to Ricky and Murphy who looked annoyed, as usual, as they stood there a moment. This would buy her some time.

"So you're definitely moving? Damn, Will and I were hoping to talk you into going out to Casper's with us tonight."

"Oh, I just heard about that place from friends of Murphy's. I guess it's a great place."

"She can't go out tonight. She has plans," Ricky stated very abruptly and Amelia was shocked. Who gave him the right to make a comment?

"I don't think I can go tonight, and tomorrow I have a party to attend. Perhaps next week?"

Paul looked at both Murphy and Ricky then back at Amelia.

"You have our numbers. Call us if you can do Saturday. I'd offer to help you move, but it looks like you have enough help," Paul said with a little bit of attitude.

"I don't have too much to move. If I can make it tonight, I'll definitely call you later."

"Really?" Paul asked as Ricky and Murphy stared at her.

"Yes. If you don't hear from me by five, then know I got caught up in moving. But I'll call you tomorrow to make plans for next week."

Paul smiled. "Great. Good luck with the move. Nice meeting you, Murphy and Ricky," Paul said then walked out of the building.

Amelia turned to watch him go until the elevator doors opened.

Then she walked into the elevator, sure that Regan and Galen were decent and pretending to cook something for lunch. She was starving.

The moment the doors closed, Ricky started. "You're not seriously interested in that guy are you?"

Amelia looked up at him. "He and his brother are nice. They work in the business offices next to the hospital."

"They're not your type at all," Ricky stated.

"Excuse me, how do you know what my type is?" she asked and then looked toward Murphy, who stared straight ahead. She noticed the vein by his temple pulsating. Then she felt Ricky's hand on her waist. The next thing she knew, he was holding her in his arms, and his thick, hard muscles were hard against her. He cupped her cheek and half her head with one large hand.

She gasped as he stared down into her eyes. She was shocked at the intensity in them and how easily he held her.

"Do they make you feel sexy and beautiful when they look at you? Does your heart race, like it is right now?"

She grabbed his arms as the elevator stopped, the bell sounded, and the doors opened. She sensed Murphy moving and she panicked that he would get to the apartment door.

"Ricky," she started to say.

"They're not for you." He lowered his mouth to hers.

He kissed her deeply, devouring her soft moans, tasting every inch of her mouth. In her mind she knew she should stop him. Push him away. Not get caught up in lustful thoughts that would only end in disaster. But he was such a good kisser. Plus, his hands were magnificent and so was his body. She felt his thigh press between her quivering thighs and she moaned into his mouth as the thick, ironclad thigh connected with her oversensitive pussy. When she felt him move his hand down her hip and to her ass, she panicked and pulled from his mouth.

She was gripping his shoulders best she could, but he was so much bigger.

"Please, you have to stop. You shouldn't have done that," she said, out of breath.

He squeezed her harder against him. She felt the long, thick, hard, ridge of his cock against her belly.

"You feel that? You know you're attracted to me, just as I am to you. That's the difference. Paul and his brother, whomever they are, can't compare."

Ricky's dominance and control should not be turning her on right now. That was her problem initially with Mano. His aggressiveness and possessiveness made her feel loved and wanted. It wasn't love. It wasn't pure and neither would this be.

She pushed him away.

"I can't get involved with you. I won't. It would never work."

"You don't know that. My brothers and I would treat you right, Amelia."

She shook her head. "Stop. Your brothers aren't interested. I'm not interested in that type of relationship."

"You were going to go out with Paul and Will. Don't lie. I can spot a liar from a mile away," Murphy stated firmly as Ricky slowly released her.

She straightened out her dress and tried to step out of the elevator but Murphy stared at her in such a way that she froze in place.

"I'm too fucking old for games. Flirting can get a woman in a heap of trouble. Trouble she may not be able to handle."

She was instantly pissed off. Big surprise there. Mad Dog Murphy did it to her every time. The nerve of him. He made her feel like a child being reprimanded by an adult. She jumped as Ricky placed his hands on her hips from behind.

"Let's get this move started and then we'll start talking about you and I going on a date."

As they walked down the hallway, she felt the anger building. This was so typical of a military man…well, men. Give orders, make demands, and expect the woman to just comply.

She pulled out her keys then looked up at Murphy and Ricky. Murphy looked about to explode and Ricky was smiling as he looked her over with hungry eyes.

Her damn fingers were shaking as she unlocked the door. Before she opened it, she looked at them.

"Neither of you have the right to give me orders. I said I'm not interested, Ricky, and, Murphy, I can flirt with whomever I damn please." As she went to open the door, Murphy covered her hand and the doorknob as he used his other hand to grab her around the waist. He stared down into her eyes and he looked determined.

"I catch you flirting again, Amelia, and I'll toss you over my knee, spank that sassy, sexy ass of yours, and stroke your wet pussy until you come, calling my name."

Holy mother of God!

His words, the tone of his voice, and the feel of his hands pressing against her ass, inches from the crack, made her almost moan. Her cheeks felt red and warm and she was sexually shocked.

"Test me, sweetheart. Please, test me and I'll do it."

She felt Murphy's hand tap her ass then move off of her as he stepped back.

The loss of his touch hit her harder than she wanted to admit. The man was such a hard-ass, disciplinary, sex god. It wasn't fair. There were two of them against her. She was so screwed.

Amelia took a deep breath and opened the door. Her wet panties reminded her of Ricky's and Murphy's effect on her with every step she took.

"Hey, you're finally here. We were waiting for you," Regan said in greeting.

Amelia felt embarrassed and hoped that Regan couldn't tell that she was sexually aroused right now.

Murphy and Ricky looked at Galen who stood by the counter in the kitchen.

"What is he doing here?" Ricky asked.

Amelia took the opportunity to make an excuse to leave. She needed to breathe. She needed to recover from that assault of sorts in the elevator and outside the door. How the hell was she going to keep her hands to herself and halt any attempt by Ricky and Murphy to make another move on her?

"I'm going to go change and then throw some last items into the boxes. I'll be back." She hurried from the room. After a glance at Murphy, she imagined him touching her the way he threatened to. And it *was* a threat. He didn't want her going out with Paul and Will. He was trying to stake a claim, but she had fallen for that once before. The heartache and loss wasn't worth the excitement and pleasure. She needed to set some rules and deny this attraction. A man, or in this case, men, who demanded possession and dominance meant trouble.

A hit from men as big as Ricky or Murphy would hurt. She should know. Mano was only an inch or so shorter and fought for a living. The thought brought tears to her eyes and made her heed caution.

Remember Mano and Escala. Remember, these type of men can not be trusted.

Chapter 6

Murphy didn't know what had come over him. Amelia got under his skin like no one else ever could. She was a secret weapon the government could use to infiltrate any male out there. Even the toughest and he thought of himself as pretty damn tough. Not ever had any woman made him so emotional. One minute he was filled with rage and the next filled with hunger. He wanted to kiss her like Ricky had. He wanted to pull her into his arms, devour any feelings of denial she may have, and explore every inch of her. The woman had a sexy, curvy body. She was not skin and bones, but softness and muscle. He didn't look at her and think he could break her, yet every part of him wanted to cherish her, caress her, make love to her. But the attraction, the desire to have Amelia was so strong. It was shockingly instant. And even now, as she unpacked what little belongings she had and bent over to lift things up, he couldn't stop his mind from imagining bending her over that couch and fucking her from behind.

The swell of her breasts accentuated by the snug-fitting camisole she wore made him stare in admiration. As he stared at the skirt she wore and imagined lifting it up and falling between her legs to take a taste of her sweet cunt, he was disappointed to see they were lined with shorts, or a skort. He thought women called them that. But he saw it as another barrier, another block from him getting what he hungered for.

He watched Ricky now, helping Amelia carry a box to her bedroom. He followed.

"How come you don't have a lot of clothes and personal items? Did you leave things at home in New York?" Ricky asked as Murphy stood by the doorway, arms crossed, leaning against the door frame.

Amelia went about pulling items out and adding them to dresser drawers.

"I don't have a home back in New York. I had an apartment but that was it. I basically left all the household items there."

"Don't women usually have a lot of clothes and shoes?" Ricky asked. "You have barely anything." It was obvious to Murphy that Ricky wasn't buying her story.

She turned to look at him then sat on the edge of the bed.

"Listen, Ricky, I have the bare necessities. Things were tough for me back in New York, which is none of your business really. I told you that I didn't need a lot of help because I don't have a lot of personal belongings."

She was filled with attitude. Murphy noticed she had been this way since leaving Regan's apartment. He had a feeling that she was attracted to them, but was fearful. He couldn't help but wonder why.

She stood up and began to walk out of the bedroom and brushed by him as she did.

The scent of her perfume and the concern in her eyes spoke volumes. He grabbed her hand to stop her and she froze in place.

She wouldn't look up at him. He felt her shaking. She was nervous.

"Darlin', we're just trying to get to know you, that's all. Don't be afraid of us. We're good men."

She slowly looked up toward him.

"Murphy, I need my privacy. I don't want to talk about New York."

He wanted to push for answers but knew he couldn't. He released her hand and followed her out to the living room. Ricky followed and walked over toward the one remaining blue plastic bin.

"What's in here?" Ricky asked as he began to undo the lid to peek inside.

"No. Don't open that." She walked over toward it.

"A secret, huh? Maybe it has some clues to what you're all about, Amelia," Ricky teased, but Amelia didn't take a liking to his brother's teasing.

"I'll take care of that one later. You guys can leave. I'll handle things from here."

Ricky pulled Amelia into his arms. "How about a little break?" He looked about ready to kiss her.

"No. No break, no fooling around, Ricky. I'm not interested."

"You didn't like my kiss before in the elevator? It seemed like you did because I sure enjoyed it."

"You're a good kisser, and you're also good at seduction, but I can't get involved with either of you."

"Why not?" Murphy asked. He didn't move closer to her. His gut warned him that something was up. But what?

"I don't date," she said then shyly turned away.

"Honey, did you forget that we were present for Paul's conversation with you?" Ricky asked.

"I don't date men like you."

Ricky raised his eyebrows and Murphy felt insulted. What the hell did she mean by that? "Men like us? You mean men that like to share their woman with their brothers and cater to her every whim?"

She swallowed hard and pulled away from Ricky. She walked a few steps away and wrapped her arms around her waist.

"I don't date men who were in the military. It's a rule I have."

There she went again, getting under his skin.

"What the hell is that supposed to mean? Are you some kind of anti-American or something? You hate soldiers? You think we're monsters?" Ricky asked, raising his voice. Murphy was glad his brother responded. His retort would have been a hell of a lot worse than that.

Amelia turned around to face the other way.

"I don't date soldiers. If it makes you feel any better, I don't date anyone who engages in fighting of any sort."

"Oh, honey, you're going to have to explain better than that. I kissed you. I felt you kiss me back. I bet if I inspected, your panties were even wet."

She turned around and shot him a dirty look.

"I'm on to you. I get it. I do. You want to control me, manipulate my mind, and make me think I'm special, and then you want to pounce. I know the MO, big-time, Ricky. Let's avoid the drama, the pain, and the bullshit and call it for what it is. I won't be you or your brother's latest fuck. Leave now."

* * * *

Amelia knew her words were harsh. She was in a panic. She liked them both. She wanted them both, but she wouldn't allow history to repeat itself. The point of making mistakes in the past was to avoid future ones. She'd been down this road. Even though it was with one man and not more than one, she knew the outcome.

"What's going on in here?"

She was shocked to see Brody, standing there with a towel, wiping his hands. She had forgotten that Murphy called him over to check out her car. Another kind act, to get her to open up her thighs. As badly as she wanted to, she knew she couldn't.

"Nothing. Your brothers were just leaving. Thanks for the help," she said then started to reach for the box. She lifted it up. It was too heavy and when Murphy went to reach for it to help her, she pulled away, lost her balance, and knocked the box over. When the lid popped open, pictures of her brother, Kyle, in uniform and the special box with a perfectly folded American flag from his funeral emerged. She knew that other pictures were in there. So were her father's and her brother Edward's flags as well that were given to her at their funerals when they died.

She looked at Murphy as he bent down next to her.

"Amelia?" he questioned.

She shook her head as she quickly pushed the items back inside and tried unsuccessfully to add the lid.

"Leave. Just leave." She stood up, leaving the box, with the lid slightly loose sitting there.

She glanced at Ricky and Brody, who now moved closer. She was shaking. She didn't want them to see those pictures and to know about her heartache. They wouldn't get it. These were her memories, her loss.

Very slowly, Murphy wrapped an arm around her waist and hoisted her up against him. She grabbed onto his forearms to try and stop him, but he was rock solid and pretty damn determined.

"Amelia, look at me."

She did instantly. His tone and his size were intimidating and initiated a natural instinctual response in her.

She locked gazes with him. She felt his other hand move up her waist then to her neck and head. He held her firmly.

"You really know how to piss a man off."

He leaned down and kissed her hard on the mouth. His tongue pushed between her teeth and a moment later she was kissing him back, allowing him complete access to her mouth and her body.

She felt his hands explore her ass and lower back as he devoured her moans and stroked the cavern of her mouth.

She never felt so aroused and needy. Hadn't she just said she didn't want them or a relationship with them?

When he lifted her up into the air and began carrying her somewhere, she panicked, pulling her mouth from his, as Murphy placed her ass on the kitchen island.

"Murphy?"

His mouth was back on hers again, stopping her from denying the attraction any further. When he finally got his fill of kissing her, he used his mouth to suckle along her neck, filling her body with goose bumps. He used one large hand to push the strap of her camisole and bra to the side and release a full breast to his mouth.

"Fucking beautiful," he whispered then suckled the nipple, causing her pussy to come alive.

"Oh God, Murphy, please. You have to stop."

"Why, when you're enjoying it and so are we," Ricky stated, instantly reminding her that they had an audience. Ricky moved in on her left and Brody on her right.

Murphy's hands were pushing up her camisole and he was caressing her ribs and belly.

She grabbed onto his head to stop him and wound up thrusting her hips up against him. He used the space to cup her ass and squeeze as he slowly released a swollen breast with a "plop."

"Delicious." He moved up to kiss her again.

"Please Murphy. We need to slow down. I told you, this can't happen," she scolded him as she held his rough skin between her hands. He had a slight shadow of a beard growing and he looked so feral and hungry as he stared at her. His face was red. His eyes sparkled as he held her gaze and cupped her bare breast. He used two fingers to tweak the nipple, and she felt her pussy weep in reaction.

"Please, Murphy. It's too much. I'm freaking out."

She felt the second set of fingers against her hairline caressing her hair from her cheeks. She glanced to the side and locked gazes with Brody.

"You're so lovely, Amelia."

She saw the sincerity in Brody's eyes, despite the way he appeared so cold and unemotional. He stared at her lips and she pulled the lower one between her bottom teeth.

He leaned forward and kissed her forehead, the bridge of her nose, and then her lips.

She lost hold of Murphy, who stepped aside only for Ricky to take his place. Brody kissed her deeply, but with passion and meaning. She felt it to her soul. But then she felt Ricky's hand cup her breast. She jerked until she felt Ricky's tongue against the tip, licking back and forth across her hardened, aroused nipple.

Amelia was in emotion overload. It was moving too fast. She needed to stop them. Brody must have sensed her concern as he released her lips then caressed her hair again.

"Nice," he whispered just as Ricky released her breast.

Ricky pulled her bra and camisole back into place then leaned forward and gave a soft kiss to her lips.

"Thank you." He helped her sit up.

"What the fuck's going on in here?"

They all turned to see Waylon standing in the doorway.

The sight of his intense stare and still-like-new bruises reminded her of her rules.

She shoved from Ricky's hold and got down off the counter.

* * * *

Murphy grabbed her hand to stop her from pushing them away.

"Whose flag was that? Who is the guy in the picture?" he asked and she gasped then hugged herself, shaking her head.

"No. You don't need to know. Please just leave."

"Leave, after that?" Brody sounded ticked off, too.

"What's going on? What guy?" Waylon asked.

"A guy in the picture. The reason why she said she doesn't date military men or men that fight," Ricky replied.

"Really? So you are a player and a flirt. You think you're too good for a soldier? Not classy enough for ya?" Waylon asked.

"You need to go. Just get your stuff and leave," she whispered.

Murphy stared at her, and when he tried to step closer, she stepped farther away.

"I don't want you here. What happened here will never happen again."

"Leave her. She's no different than the others. I don't know why you even wasted your time with her." Waylon turned around and left first. Brody shook his head and walked after him and Ricky looked her over then looked at Murphy.

"Go ahead. I'll be right there," Murphy told him, and Ricky walked out.

"I don't know what ideas are running through your head, woman. My brothers and I haven't given another woman the time of day in years. You come along, and well, you did something to each of us." She looked up at him, her eyes as big as saucers and filled with unshed tears.

"Patience sure as shit ain't one of the Haas family traits. I'll leave this alone for now, but eventually, I'm gonna find out the truth. I always do."

"Leave, Murphy. Please, just leave."

He gave her a wink then walked out of the cottage, closing the door behind him.

As he headed toward his truck and his brothers' trucks, he shook his head.

They looked angry.

"Just leave her be. In time, she'll open up. Let's head home."

Chapter 7

"See, I told you that you would have a good time, Amelia," Regan said then tipped her shot glass against Amelia's and Velma's. They swallowed them down as the group of Velma's friends and some rowdy cowboys hooted and hollered.

Amelia could feel the buzz. She hadn't drank like this ever before. She wasn't drunk yet, but if she kept up with Regan, she was going to have a hell of a hangover for the family party tomorrow.

Thoughts of that brought thoughts of her brothers. She'd practically cried her eyes out all afternoon.

Now here they were having an awesome time celebrating Velma's twenty-first birthday which started Friday night.

Amelia was standing up and moved to the right as one of Velma's guy friends came up to give her a birthday kiss. A moment later, Amelia felt the hands on her hips. Someone was pressing up against her back.

"This is quite the surprise."

Paul.

"Paul. What are you doing here?" She turned around to face him and his brother Will. Will placed his hand on her waist, too, and leaned forward to kiss her cheek hello. She turned and accidently caused his lips to touch hers.

"You look hot, Amelia," he said, looking her over.

"Thank you." She had borrowed the dress from Regan and even though the strapless top was a bit smaller than she would have liked, Velma and Regan talked her into wearing it.

It was tight up top, flared out toward the bottom, and the little fringe on the end danced against her thighs as she walked. It was red and very sexy, but loose enough to dance in and feel comfortable.

Paul kept a hand on her lower back and Will kept one on her waist as they talked with her.

"Hey, guys, how's it going?" Regan asked Paul and Will, then laid her head on Amelia's shoulder.

Amelia could tell that Regan was feeling the alcohol. Every time Amelia, Regan, and Velma walked up to the bar someone brought them a drink or a shot.

"We're doing great, honey. Looks like you're having fun," Paul said then looked at Will and winked.

Amelia picked up on it as Paul pushed a strand of hair from Regan's cheek.

"You look hot tonight, Regan," he told her and she giggled then pulled her head off of Amelia's shoulder. Placing her hands on her hips she scolded Paul.

"Don't you start flirting with me. I'm taken. I know you and your brother want Amelia."

"Regan." Amelia shook her head. Regan turned around and placed her arm over her sister's shoulder.

Will pulled Amelia closer to him, then leaned down to whisper against her ear. "Don't get upset with Regan. You know what she said is true. Come home with us tonight."

She closed her eyes and absorbed the feel of both men touching her. Will was caressing her back as he lay soft kisses against her ear and Paul was rubbing her left arm. He was caressing it up and down, letting his hand glide against the swell of her breast. She wanted to feel something. Or perhaps she didn't want to feel at all. She was so angry about what happened today with the Haas brothers. Yet, she missed their presence when they left. She pushed them away. She insisted that they go and that they not pursue her. But, standing here now, feeling the burn of the alcohol move through her body, combined with Paul and Will touching her, basically telling her they wanted to have sex, did absolutely nothing for her.

They didn't come close to Murphy's, Ricky's, or Brody's touch. They didn't get under her skin and make her panties wet like the commanding tone Waylon had. As much as she wanted to fight her attraction, she wasn't certain she could.

"Want to leave now, or do you want to stay for Velma's party a little longer?" Will asked.

She should just go with them. The Haas brothers were all wrong for her. They would gain control over her. In fact they already did control her, affect her, and get to her. She wanted them. She fantasized about having them and belonging to them, but she knew she would only get hurt in the end. She wasn't a slut either, and she wouldn't sleep with Will and Paul, two men she didn't know, just to try to get four other men out of her head. She chuckled.

"What's so funny?" Paul asked.

She swallowed hard then looked up into his eyes. Taking a step back, causing them to release her, she smiled.

"I'm sorry. I'm not that type of woman. I don't know either of you." Paul looked upset and so did Will, but then they glanced at one another then back at her. Will took her hand and brought it up to his lips. He kissed the top.

"Then get to know us. Sorry we were so forward. Let's enjoy the party and then we can work on setting up some dates." He smiled.

"It will be torture, but we'll do it, for you," Paul added and winked. She smiled.

* * * *

"What the hell is going on out there?" Waylon asked Murphy.

"Sounds like a bunch of teenage girls screaming and having a party," Murphy stated.

The noises of truck doors slamming, girls squealing, and water splashing down by the lake awoke all of them. Their house was the closest to the lake and a good distance from the main house and Amelia's cottage.

That thought instantly upset Waylon. He didn't get Amelia at all. He wanted to know her secrets. He wanted to know why she pushed his brothers away like she did and who the hell the soldier was who died.

"I'm going to go check it out," Murphy said and Waylon decided to join him.

As they exited the house, they saw Ricky and Brody. They were shaking their heads.

"What's going on?" Murphy asked.

"Oh, they're all pretty drunk," Ricky stated, laughing.

Waylon watched as some people went skinny-dipping and others stripped down to their panties and bras. He searched for Amelia and found her immediately. He and his brothers moved closer. The moonlight illuminated the water and the short beach around it. Clothes were spread about, and there were more girls than guys.

Amelia had her arms crossed and was standing there wearing a sexy red dress, that accentuated her every curve. The high heels showed off her defined calves and thighs. She looked sexy.

"Come on, Amelia! Just pull it off and jump in. We're all naked," Regan yelled and everyone cheered. A few guys, including Galen, were in the water, too. It pissed him off that they stopped to see Amelia undress.

"Those fuckers are watching her," Murphy stated.

"The hell they're not." Waylon began to walk toward Amelia to stop her. She moved her hands to the hem of her dress and slowly began to wiggle free. Inch by inch she pulled the tight red material up over her perfectly round ass then over her head. Waylon froze in place.

She wore black thong bikini panties and a black lace strapless bra.

He couldn't move. He was in awe of her body. Was that a tattoo on her hip?

"Hot damn, woman!" someone yelled and then the others all started. He was too late. They all saw Amelia.

She raised her arms, accentuating her breasts as they pushed forward. Her belly dipped inward, her hips more defined in the moonlight, as she adjusted her hair atop of her head.

She kicked off her high heels, and ran into the water.

Everyone screamed and cheered.

Waylon was totally pissed off.

His brothers joined him. They watched and waited, as each wild partier got out of the water. One by one, they shook and shivered, realizing that they didn't have any towels.

Galen lifted Regan up into his arms and carried her off to his truck. Velma and her friends grabbed their clothes and headed toward the fire they'd built near the bunkhouse closer to the main house. The others gathered around followed.

"Come on, Amelia. Join us," some guys yelled to her and she shook her head.

"I'm going to go change."

"We can help you," one guy and his two buddies offered and Waylon looked at Murphy.

"We got her," Murphy stated firmly and the three men immediately turned around and ran to catch up with the others.

Amelia looked up and appeared shocked to see them.

Ricky held her dress.

"What would you have done if those men followed you back to the cottage?" Waylon reprimanded her.

She shivered then stared straight up at him. As she went to place her hands on her hips, she teetered slightly and he knew she had been drinking. Her breasts moved with the motion and his dick grew even harder than it was from her earlier striptease.

"Give me my dress, Ricky."

"No," Ricky said.

"The shoes and dress are Regan's. I borrowed them," she slurred.

"Let's get you inside and dried off," Brody stated.

"No. I can do it myself. Although Waylon doesn't think I can take care of myself." She began to walk and nearly tripped. Waylon grabbed her hips to steady her. Her skin was ice cold. If they didn't get her warmed up, she would have a serious cold by morning.

"Come on. Let's walk together."

"No. I'm not falling for your seductive charms. Not any of you. If I wanted company in my bed tonight, then I would have gone home with Paul and Will when they asked me to," she blurted out then began to walk.

Waylon heard his brothers curse, and he was instantly pissed off as he lowered his shoulder and lifted Amelia up off of the ground. She bounced on top of his shoulder as he turned and headed toward her cottage.

"Put me down, Waylon."

He ignored her and her complaints of dizziness as she slapped his ass, his thighs, and bare back. He hadn't even bothered to put a shirt on, just his jeans as he and his brothers headed outside.

They got to her cottage and he opened the door. It was unlocked.

"You left your door unlocked. Those men could have—"

Murphy slammed the door closed behind them.

Waylon slowly lowered Amelia's feet to the floor. She swayed a moment and he bent down to keep his hands on her hips to steady her. She was only about five feet four inches tall. Now standing here, bare foot and practically naked, she appeared so feminine and petite surrounded by him and his brothers. They were all over six feet tall and muscular.

He stared at the cleavage of her large breasts, then her firm, taut belly, and of course the sexy tattoo. It was a floral design on a vine over her hip bone. It dipped toward her panties and he felt the tinge of jealousy for the tattoo artist that worked so close to her pussy. It was weird.

As he stared at the design, he noticed the darker center to one of the flowers, but then Amelia moved her hands to push his off of her.

"I can stand on my own, Waylon. I'm not that drunk," she slurred and then turned and nearly fell. Murphy was right behind her, holding a towel to wrap her in.

He covered her and she snuggled into the warm towel as Murphy lifted her up and against him.

"What are you doing?" she asked in a panic.

"Taking you to bed."

"You're going to take advantage of me aren't you? It figures. All you soldiers are alike," she stated, and Waylon looked at Ricky and Brody. They all wondered what she meant.

"We're not all alike and we're not going to take advantage of you. Now, I'm going to hold the towel and you're going to take off these wet things."

She stared up at him, as if he were lying.

"I promise, we won't look." He set her down and arranged the towel in front of her like a curtain. He turned his head. "At least not tonight."

She growled as she took off her wet panties and bra.

Waylon swallowed hard. This was torture. He wanted her, she didn't want them, and knowing that other guys tried to seduce her into bed tonight angered him.

Murphy wrapped the towel around her.

"Okay, you can all leave now. I'm fine." She sat down on the bed.

"Are you sure? You don't feel sick or dizzy?" Murphy asked.

"No. What do you think I'm like fifteen and it's the first time I had a few too many drinks? Please just go. I can take care of myself." They were about to leave when she stood up and leaned forward to get something from the drawer. She bumped into the table, knocked over the lamp, and the towel fell from her body.

Thank God Murphy moved into action. Waylon and his brothers couldn't move.

They watched as Murphy lifted her up and placed her in bed. He pulled the sheets and covers up to her chest then sat on the side of her.

"Now, no more moving around or you could get hurt. We're leaving now. We'll talk tomorrow."

She pulled the covers tighter and nodded her head.

"Sorry. I guess I might have had a few too many shots. It's been forever since I loosened up." She closed her eyes and leaned into the pillow.

Murphy caressed her hair from her cheek and sat there staring at her.

"I'll be fine. You can go," she whispered, sounding as if she were already beginning to doze off.

"Are you sure? One of us could stay."

"I'm okay. I don't let men I don't know stay with me. That's why I said no to Paul and Will," she said, waving her hand in the air then dropping it back to the bed. Waylon could see the swell of her breast from where she lay. The covers were nearly to her areola.

He watched as she adjusted her head and sighed.

"Is that the only reason why you said no to them?" Murphy asked as he continued to caress her hair and cheek.

She shook her head against the pillow.

"Then why else?" he asked her.

"'Cause of the Haas brothers," she mumbled and then fell to sleep.

Waylon felt his stomach tighten.

They walked out of the bedroom.

* * * *

"I don't think we should leave her alone tonight," Murphy stated.

"I'll stay. She could get up and fall or something during the night. I don't feel right leaving her," Waylon said.

"I understand. I don't think she'll remember what she said when the morning comes," Murphy added.

"Sure as shit will deny it entirely," Ricky said then chuckled.

"She said no to them. She was thinking about us. It doesn't matter if she'll remember admitting that. She said it and that gives me hope," Brody said then walked out of the house.

"I'll come over first thing in the morning. We'll make some breakfast," Ricky said then exited the house next.

Murphy stared at Waylon.

"You sure that you don't want me to stay? She may be pretty pissed off come morning."

"I couldn't sleep now if I tried. Come over in the morning."

"Okay," Murphy said then walked out.

Waylon locked the door then walked over toward her bedroom again.

He stared at her as she slept.

He felt the struggle within himself, the fight to not get involved with her or any woman and the need to feel. He was a coldhearted bastard. He knew that. He took his anger, his frustration, and emotions out in the ring. Right now, he wanted to hit something. It was how he dealt with the memories of his past. The way he blurred the images in his head of all the bodies, the loss, the danger of being Special Forces. That hollow feeling in the pit of his stomach never left him. Since the time he and Brody were orphaned and left to fend for themselves, there was that emptiness. He tried so hard to fill it with obsession of the job, being the best he could be in Special Forces, and even now in the ring.

Over the years he and Brody talked about that emptiness, and strived to fill it with all the wrong things. No woman, no bonds between comrades could fill it. It was always there. Always lingering as a reminder of his inadequacies. His parents hadn't even wanted him and Brody. Thank God for the dads and Mom.

He shook his head, wondering why the hell all these thoughts were hitting him right now. He walked away from her and toward the large, long sofa. He would never fit on it. He would be sore by morning, but he wasn't leaving her. He couldn't get himself to shut her out. He didn't know why, but he hoped that he could get to the bottom of this and find out why Amelia was so adamant about him and his brothers.

He had another week before his next fight in Dallas. He needed to train, starting Monday.

He pulled out his cell phone and looked over his calendar. A picture of him from one of the fights in Vegas appeared in an e-mail from his trainer.

He stared at the picture, and the fierce expression. He looked like a monster, a man of steel. In the ring he felt free. In the ring nothing else mattered and as he fought his opponent, that hollow feeling slightly filled. It wasn't totally gone, but it mended temporarily as he fought to exhaustion.

Yeah, in the ring, I'm numb to everything.

Chapter 8

Amelia lay in bed staring at the ceiling. Considering that she was feeling pretty good last night, she didn't have a huge headache. She wondered why she was naked in bed, then sort of remembered Murphy talking with her after Waylon carried her half naked from the lake.

Her cheeks warmed with embarrassment.

She slowly got up and pulled on a pair of boy short panties and a camisole. She walked to the bathroom, washed her face, brushed her teeth, and pulled her hair from the confines of some crazy updo. She remembered pulling her hair up to avoid getting wet when she jumped into the lake in her panties and bra.

She'd shown off her body to a bunch of strangers. She'd definitely had a few too many.

She decided that coffee would help clear her head before she took a shower. She walked through the hallway and into the kitchen, halting as she saw the large, shirtless man standing there.

She gasped and Waylon turned around to face her.

He looked her over and widened his eyes.

"Morning."

"Uhm, what are you doing here?"

He turned on the pot of coffee then walked closer. The man had a gorgeous chest. It was lightly dusted with hair that led down to his jeans. He was so defined. She gulped in appreciation of his sculptured body. He was a boxer and had a rigorous workout routine. She knew enough about that from Mano.

The thought placed a heap of fear into her gut as she turned to look away.

"You were kind of out of it last night. My brothers and I were worried that you could hurt yourself during the night," he said then looked at her from head to toe. Instantly her nipples hardened, and she realized she shouldn't be standing here half naked.

He looked her over again. "You make it a habit of walking around in your panties?"

"No, I don't. But then, this is my place, isn't it?" she asked with attitude then walked around the island, away from him, and reached up to grab two mugs for the coffee.

"I appreciate you staying. It wasn't necessary."

"I thought otherwise." They held one another's gaze.

"I don't need a babysitter, Waylon."

"You did last night."

"Really?"

"Sure did. You stripped down to your thong panties and bra that covered hardly anything in front of a bunch of drunk cowboys. You're lucky we were there."

She slammed her hand down on the counter then stalked toward him.

"Get out, Waylon. I don't sleep around."

There was a knock at the door, but before she could move, Waylon grabbed a hold of her camisole and pulled her toward him. He lifted her up, placed her onto the counter, and pressed his body between her thighs. She grabbed onto his shoulders, and now was almost face-to-face. He still towered over her.

His hand moved behind her head as he gripped her hard.

"You need looking after. You're not going to flaunt this sexy body all over town."

"I can do whatever I want to do," she retorted and he ground his teeth before he pulled her closer and kissed her hard on the mouth.

In a matter of seconds he was shoving his tongue between her teeth, and they were battling for control of the kiss.

He made love to her mouth like no one ever had before. He was relentless in his strokes, combined with the exploration of his hands.

She grabbed onto his shoulders, raised her knees, and pressed them against his ribs. His hand grabbed her ass und squeezed her toward him. She ran the palms of her hands up and over his biceps, his shoulder and neck, feeling the power and the muscles beneath her fingers.

In the distance she heard the door close and she knew his brothers were there and her pussy clenched then released her arousal. She moaned into Waylon's mouth and tried to pull back. He wouldn't allow it. He held her head and face between both hands and continued to kiss her until she could hardly breathe. When he finally released her lips, they were both panting for air.

He stared at her with frustration in his eyes. "You drive me fucking crazy."

"You started it."

"I finished it."

She tried to push him away and get down off the counter, but he wouldn't allow it. He held her by her hips. He maneuvered his fingers beneath her boy shorts and caressed her inner groin with his thick, hard thumbs.

She gasped.

"Someone feeling sassy this morning?"

She turned to see Murphy and Ricky. Her heart raced. Then she wondered where Brody was. She sought him out, too. *What the hell?*

"Your brother thinks I need a babysitter," she stated with attitude, but never took her gaze from Waylon's.

"You sure did last night," Ricky said.

Waylon raised his eyebrows to her as if saying, "I told you so."

She tried again, unsuccessfully, to get down.

Waylon pulled her harder against him and off the counter. He was carrying her to her room.

"What are you doing? Where are you taking me?"

He didn't answer as she struggled between being fully aroused by the man's audacity and dominance and being resistant to what might happen. She couldn't get involved with them. *But maybe I could have a little fun with them. No! No, don't be so foolish. You already have feelings for them, you idiot.*

"Waylon, let me down."

She squealed as he dropped her to the bed. She bounced, but before she could get control of her position, he knelt onto the bed between her legs and pulled her underneath him. He hung over her. One hand pressed against the comforter and her left ear and the other by her waist. His knee was wedged snug against her crotch and his foot was on the floor for support.

He stared down into her eyes and she remained perfectly still. His expression was priceless. *Holy fuck, he's lethally hot.*

* * * *

Waylon stared at the sexy minx before him. Her camisole was pushed all the way up, her breasts peeking out from the sides of the flimsy material. He stared at her body, her luscious, sexy, curvy figure and practically growled with possessiveness. He'd never felt so carnal over a woman. It was like she stirred some sort of beast within him. Her scent, her body, her complete femininity aroused every sense in his body.

He moved a hand along her hip bone making her jerk slightly. But she didn't move away. She remained still.

He trailed one finger along the tattoo.

"When did you get this?" he asked as she parted her wet lips and took an uneasy breath.

"Last year."

"It's beautiful, like you."

He used his finger to follow the lines of the vine choosing an upward motion until his fingers brushed against the large swell of her breast.

"Waylon?"

"Shhh, not a word, Amelia. I'm so angry with you right now, and your damn hard-as-stone attitude. The thought of you stripping last night in front of those drunk cowboys makes me feel jealous and angry."

He trailed his finger down her body, following the thin line of the vines, noticing the raised skin beneath one of the flowers. He continued to move lower, and when he pressed under her panties, Amelia stopped him.

"Waylon, I told you that this can't happen."

He held her gaze.

"That was before you kissed me the way you did. I'm not going to hurt you."

"That's why we can't do this. We can't get involved. I don't want that."

"What is it that you're so afraid of? Who hurt you so badly that you'd lump up all soldiers and fighters in one category to stay clear of? Who?" he asked, raising his voice.

"Waylon!" They turned toward the doorway. It was Murphy.

"Brody called. Velma is missing. She wasn't in the cottage this morning with her friends."

"Oh God," Amelia said.

"Come on. We'll finish this later." Waylon offered her a hand and she took it. He pulled her up and against him, instantly spreading his hand over her ass. He gave it a squeeze as he held her gaze.

"You go get dressed and we'll talk later."

"Waylon, I told you—"

He pressed a finger over her lips to stop her from talking. "Later, Amelia."

He walked out into the living room.

"Where are we going to look first?" he asked his brothers.

"The dads are pissed. We'll meet over there at the main house," Murphy said and they gave Amelia a look.

"I'll come, too."

"No, you shower and dress. One of us will come back for you," Waylon stated then gave her a look. She placed her hands on her hips and was about to give him shit, but instead he turned and walked out with his brothers. He could practically feel her eyes burning him with curses under her breath. Now she would know how she made him feel.

He chuckled as he walked out with his brothers.

"You think she'll listen?" Ricky asked.

"Hell no," both Murphy and Waylon said at the same time and they all laughed.

* * * *

Amelia couldn't believe it. She took a shower, got dressed in a cute sundress, and debated about leaving for the main house or listening to Waylon's order. That was exactly what it was, too. An order. It was a show of control that she wasn't biting on or accepting. Yet, what pissed her off entirely more than his nerve was the fact that she stood there waiting for the last thirty minutes coming up with one excuse after the next to wait for him.

She growled as she made fists by her side.

Her cell phone rang and she walked over to answer it.

"Hey, come over to the main house. Velma just got here and my brothers and dads are pissed."

"Are you sure, Regan? This may be a family thing."

"Amelia, come here please."

"I'm on my way." She hung up the phone, grabbed her purse, and walked out the door, locking it before she left. She couldn't help but feel guilty for leaving. Apparently Waylon had a way of getting to her mind. The man got under her skin. All four of them did. Well, maybe not Brody. He was so quiet and serious all the time. She wondered why, as she started her car and headed toward the main house. As she pulled up, she saw all the trucks and SUV, plus other vehicles. Today was supposed to be the big family party. Guests would be arriving in two hours.

Amelia parked her car then walked toward the front steps. Regan greeted her and took her hand, leading her toward the family room.

"You look tired," Amelia told Regan.

"Hungover is more like it. Come on. Something is up and Velma isn't budging. Wherever she was, she wasn't alone. If you know what I mean."

"Oh boy."

"Exactly."

As they approached, Amelia could hear their fathers asking Velma to explain where she was and why she didn't tell anyone. Elise, expressed concern over her well-being and her brothers just stood there with their arms crossed in front of their massive chests. Talk about intimidation? These men were a force field and then some.

"I told you, I was with friends. I drank a little too much and woke up thirty minutes ago. No big deal," Velma stated.

"It is a big deal. We got your brothers and their friends to search for you. The police were starting to organize a search party," Tysen stated firmly.

"Please. I wasn't even gone twenty-four hours. Aren't there rules?"

"Watch the attitude, Velma," Murphy stated.

Amelia walked into the room with Regan, and everyone looked at her. They said hello and she responded to their parents and mom, but didn't look at the brothers. They were too angry right now. She did look at Velma and there was definitely something going on. Perhaps she snuck out with a guy? There were some pretty good-looking cowboys hanging around her last night. But then she noticed the bruise on her arm and a large scratch.

"Okay. I can see we're getting nowhere with this. Guests are going to be arriving soon. Why don't you go shower, think things over, then talk to us and explain tonight. That should give you plenty of time to remember," Elise said then rose from the chair and walked out of the room. She was wearing an apron, and as she passed Amelia, she placed her hand on her arm.

"Can you help me with that stuffed mushroom recipe, honey?"

"Sure thing," Amelia said. She had completely forgotten about giving Regan's mom the recipe. Regan's dads smiled at her as they left the room. Amelia was about to follow Regan and Velma upstairs to Velma's bedroom when someone wrapped an arm around her waist from behind.

Waylon pulled her back against him. She grabbed onto his thick, muscular forearm, amazed at how hard it was. "Didn't I tell you to stay put until I came for you?" he whispered next to her ear. Murphy, Ricky, and Brody stood around them.

"Didn't I tell you that you're not the boss of me?"

He squeezed her a little tighter and she felt the ridge of his thick, hard cock against her lower back. It infused the fact that he was a big man and tall, too.

"Come with me outside to the barn."

"No."

He kissed along her neck then over her ear. "Yes. Come with me. There's something we need to talk about."

She sighed in annoyance.

"Regan asked me to come here right away. I think she wants me to talk to Velma, too."

"They can wait. Velma is stubborn."

"It must run in the family," she said and Ricky chuckled.

Waylon kissed her neck then released his hold. Before she could move, Murphy pulled her toward him. He placed his hands on her hips and stared down into her eyes.

"What is it with you and sexy, little dresses?"

"This isn't sexy." She felt Ricky move in behind her. He ran his hands along her arms and let his fingers caress against the side of her breasts on either side. She tightened up, as she felt her body react to their touch. They knew just what to do to get her aroused.

"With an ass like yours, Amelia, every outfit looks sexy." He moved a hand along her neck to grip her hair ever so lightly. She felt his possessive move and turned to reprimand him, catching his lips as they descended upon hers.

He kissed her softly but pressed his tongue between her teeth. As she absorbed the way Ricky tasted and how he held her head and hair, she realized how turned on she was. Denying this attraction was useless. But what about her past? What about Mano and the fighting?

The sound of their father Sam's voice coming from the kitchen caused Ricky to release her lips and step away. Murphy reached out and caressed her lower lip with his thumb.

"You look really pretty, Amelia. Are you wearing a pair of those sexy little thongs of yours?" Murphy asked.

He was so commanding and bossy. She immediately thought of a drill sergeant or some other kind of really intense demanding instructor. He was at least ten years older than her. He could have his choice of any woman, any age he wanted. They all could.

"That's none of your business, Murphy." He shook his head at her.

"Oh, I'm making it my business."

Her belly felt as if it dropped to her knees.

"Murphy! Leave Amelia alone. I need her," Regan yelled from the top of the stairs, but Murphy hadn't budged.

He gave Amelia a tap to her waist.

"See you in a little bit," he said, and Amelia walked toward the stairs, brushing her shoulders between Brody and Waylon as she passed by. Brody just stared at her.

She hurried toward the stairs to Regan who winked then grabbed her arm and pulled her upstairs.

"My sister is in a bit of a pickle."

"What's up?"

"You'll see. So what's with my brothers? Did you sleep with them last night?"

"Regan!"

"What? They like you, you like them. There you go. It's human nature."

"Not for me it isn't."

"Oh, well, they'll convince you and then you'll be my sister-in-law."

"Regan, stop!"

Regan laughed as she laid her head on Amelia's shoulder. For a moment Amelia wondered if Regan were teasing.

When they entered the large bedroom, Velma was looking at herself in the mirror. Amelia saw the bandage on her arm.

"What happened?"

"She said she fell against something hard and sharp in the lake last night. I'm not buying it."

Amelia walked closer and took Velma's arm to inspect the bruising and scrape.

"Are you okay?" she asked and Velma nodded as tears filled her eyes.

"Well, Mom needs some help downstairs," Regan stated.

"I thought you said that you needed my help up here?" Amelia asked.

"Oh, I was just trying to give you some space from my brothers. They were practically feeling you up in the front entryway."

"Oh my God, they like Amelia. They made a move?"

"Moves," Amelia said then shook her head.

Regan and Velma fist pumped into the air.

"Hey."

"Hey what, Amelia? Our brothers have never even brought a woman home. They're so hard and critical and damn annoying with their control issues. They definitely like you or they wouldn't be following you everywhere you go," Regan said.

"Waylon picked her up and tossed her over his shoulder last night. They walked her to her cottage," Velma said.

"Hot damn, woman," Regan stated, shaking her hand in front of her as if too hot to contemplate the vision.

"Nothing happened."

"It will tonight. They want you and they always get what they want. Those are the type of men they are," Regan stated.

"What are you afraid of, Amelia?" Velma asked.

"Everything. All four of them. Their muscles, their fighting abilities, and the fact that they were in the service. Their commanding attitudes and forcefulness and mostly, their fists."

"Their fists?" Regan asked.

Amelia nodded. "I didn't exactly tell you everything about my life back in New York. Now isn't the time either. Your mom needs help. But what I will tell you, is that I got involved with the wrong man. Things got out of hand. Moving here was a risk, but also a necessity."

"He hit you, Amelia?" Velma asked, and Amelia nodded.

"Many times. It was bad and he was big."

"Shit, Amelia. How the hell did this happen? What about your brothers?" Regan asked.

"I don't want to talk about it."

The phone on the table rang and Regan walked over to answer it. Amelia locked gazes with Velma.

"I'm sorry that happened. I sort of got into some trouble recently with a guy. He showed up last night."

"What? Did he hurt you?"

Velma nodded her head. "I stopped him before things got out of control and then he shoved me and I fell. I scraped my arm."

"You should call the police and press charges."

"No need to. I had help last night." Velma smiled as her cheeks turned red.

"Another man?"

She nodded her head.

"Well, tell me."

Velma looked toward her sister who was obviously talking to one of their dads. Regan was saying that they would be down shortly.

"As Mark was being aggressive and threatening, Jonas showed up. He had been watching me from a distance all night and joined us at the lake. I had no idea he was even around, but thank God he followed us. When Mark grabbed me, Jonas intervened and needless to say, Mark got his ass kicked."

"Nice. Then what happened?"

Velma lowered her eyes and clasped her hands together. "Jonas and I spent the night together. We didn't have sex, but we might as well have. He was really sweet and told me that he had been waiting for me to notice him. He's just a bit concerned about my brothers' and fathers' reactions. He's worked on the ranch for years and does his own wood carving business on the side. I like him and it felt so right with him. You know?"

"I know. That's great. Is he coming here tonight?"

"I sure hope so. I told him that I would talk to my dads and mom today. That's what I need to do now. Plus, he has two brothers. Apparently, they're interested, too."

"Wow. I'm glad that you were safe and he helped you. You be sure to let someone know if that Mark guy comes around again. Men like that never give up easily. Are you certain about meeting Jonas's brothers? Is that the kind of relationship you want?"

"I know I like Jonas a lot. It was so instant. I never felt anything like this before, Amelia. I'm going to meet them and see what happens. If the same chemistry isn't there, then so be it. Jonas is really great. Now, how about you? You know, you can trust my brothers. They would never hit you."

Amelia raised her hand. "I couldn't handle the fear I have being with one of them their size, never mind four. I think I'll focus on work for now. That should keep me out of trouble."

Velma shook her head. "You can keep denying your attraction all you want. They'll get you to come around. They like you and that's saying a lot. My brothers are very private men. They have a lot of pain in their hearts, Amelia. That's something you share in common with them. Just keep an open mind. If it happens, then so be it."

Regan got off the phone and joined them.

"Are we ready?" Regan asked and Amelia looked at Velma. She smiled and nodded her head.

As they headed downstairs, Amelia couldn't help but feel a bit nervous. They walked into the kitchen and helped Elise with some last-minute prework. They were laughing and enjoying themselves when Regan heard Amelia's cell phone ringing.

Amelia picked up her purse as the women headed outside to greet the guests.

Amelia didn't recognize the number so she let it go to voice mail. She waited until the message was recorded and heard the phone beep.

As she placed the phone to her ear, she felt the instant fear and panic hit her insides.

"Amelia! Fucking Texas, huh? Why? Is that where you've been hiding out for the past year? You come to the city and visit the neighborhood, talk and flirt with my brother, then take off again? You should know by now that I have connections. Next time I call, pick up the fucking phone or I'll fly out there and drag your ass back here. We need to talk. You can't run from me, from us, forever."

Amelia felt a mix of emotions. She was scared, she was angry, but mostly afraid.

"Amelia, are you okay?"

Amelia turned to the right and saw Regan's dad, Sam. He was watching her and he had a scowl on his face. She wiped the tear that nearly fell from her eye.

"Oh, yes, fine, thank you." She placed the phone into the small bag and pulled it off the counter. He stepped closer.

"Bad news?" he asked.

She looked at him strangely.

"The phone call? You were listening to a call when I came in. You didn't even hear me."

"Oh, it was nothing." She looked down and took an unsteady breath.

"Amelia, if something is wrong, you can tell me or even Elise."

"It's nothing I can't handle. Just a surprise call. I appreciate your kind gesture."

He smiled at her. "Go on outside, the music is getting started and Elise is quite the dancer." He winked and Amelia forced a smile as she walked outside along with Sam. She felt her body shaking, but tried to pretend that her mind wasn't on Mano or New York.

Many people showed up for the bash and Amelia couldn't help but to watch the Haas men cater to their wife Elise. She wished life could be so simple. She couldn't help but wonder if Mano would have the audacity to come out here. She knew he would. He was resourceful, and now he was rich. She had evaded him and his brother for a year, spending her time outside of the city in upstate New York. He called her a few times and she had her phone number changed. She couldn't do that now. She needed it for work and she didn't want the hassle. No, she would have to talk to him and make him understand that things were over. That it had been his fault and she was starting a new life. It was the only way.

* * * *

The party was a success. Elise watched as her sons showed total and obvious interest in Amelia. She had to laugh as Amelia kept trying to sidestep away from one of them or simply swat at their hands as they sneakily stroked her hip. She knew that feeling. The overwhelming sense of embarrassment for being publically exposed like that, yet completely aroused by the attention. Her own men, Sam, Jordan, and Tysen, had been like that. In fact, they still placed her first and always made sure she was happy and provided for.

Elise watched her sons. They had hard lives, especially Brody and Waylon. She'll never forget their dirty, sad faces the first days they'd shown up around the ranch to help out for money or just food. It broke her heart knowing that their parents abandoned them. The decision to adopt them was instant and she knew in her heart that it was the right thing to do. She'd never regretted it. Not even when the boys got into some trouble now and again.

She chuckled to herself.

The crew of them were so much alike that they did everything together. They even joined the service. She sighed at that memory. They'd changed some after those eight years. Brody and Waylon had changed the most.

She watched now as Brody placed his hand on Amelia's waist as she spoke to Velma and Jonas. It was about time Jonas made a move. He'd liked Velma for a long time.

"What are you staring at so intently?" Sam asked as he came up behind Elise, wrapping his arms around her. She placed her hands over his and leaned back against his chest. She loved the feel of being in her men's arms. She felt safest and most loved there.

"I was just watching our son's act blatantly possessive of Amelia. They're making it clear that they like her."

"Hmm, I did notice that. She seems resistant, doesn't she?"

"Oh, I wouldn't quite say resistant, as I would cautious. I can recall meeting you, Jordan, and Tysen, and trying to get used to your public displays of possession."

He laughed as his warm breath caressed against her skin. She closed her eyes and smiled. She felt his lips kiss her skin by her ear.

"Damn straight we did. Wanted every man in the vicinity to know you were taken. Those boys are definitely making their intentions known. I just hope they don't push too much. Amelia is very quiet and only learned of ménage relationships from Regan."

"You think she's not interested?"

"I wouldn't say that. She likes all four of them. I've never seen Brody, Waylon, or Murphy pay so much attention to a woman. Ricky on the other hand, he's got some personality."

Elise laughed. Ricky flirted a bunch, but he'd never brought a woman home to the ranch. That said a lot right there.

"I'm not sure if it's anything to be concerned about, but earlier, Amelia got a phone call and she looked pretty shaken up. I walked into the kitchen and she hadn't even heard me. There were tears in her eyes, and when I asked her if things were okay, she of course said she was fine. I could tell she wasn't." Elise turned around to face Sam.

"Could something be wrong and she's not telling us or Regan? She has been on her own for years. Regan mentioned Amelia losing everything she had."

Sam scowled.

"What do you mean?"

"My understanding is that she had to sell off the house and belongings to pay for funeral expenses. Regan wouldn't say much more. She only mentioned Amelia living in a place in the country for a year by cooking meals in between working at a hospital. I don't really know the details."

"Well, if there is something wrong, perhaps accepting our sons' attention will give her the confidence to confide in them."

"I hope they really do like her. I'd be disappointed in them and pretty angry if they hurt that young woman."

"They won't. Like you said, we've never seen any of them act like this before and definitely not all four, together."

Sam squeezed her shoulders and Elise smiled, hoping that her sons and daughters would find love as wonderful, perfect, and strong as her and her husbands'.

* * * *

Amelia finished washing some dishes in the sink when she felt the arm wrap around her waist from behind. She jumped, dropping the dishtowel as strong arms embraced her.

"Come with me."

Brody.

"Where?" she asked, immediately feeling aroused and nervous. Brody was so quiet and fierce looking all the time. His seriousness caused these tiny wrinkles above the bridge of his nose and between his eyebrows. He was very tan, like his brothers and just as tall as Murphy and Waylon.

She hesitated until he turned her around to face him. He pressed her back against the counter and sink and stared down into her eyes. *God, he's so beautiful.*

He reached up and trailed his index finger along her jaw. She parted her lips, suddenly feeling almost breathless from the attraction between them. She felt his muscular hand glide across her neck, under her hairline and to the base of her head, tilting her head back.

"I like this dress," he said so very seriously she didn't know if it were a compliment. This was Brody. He was hard, stern, quiet, and yet his touch was gentle and unexpected.

"Me, too," she whispered.

He leaned down, and before he lowered his lips to hers, she closed her eyes.

"Yes," he whispered before he kissed her. It made her think that he wasn't so sure that she would let him. A man so big, so commanding and sexy felt insecure around her? How outrageous. She was the insecure one. She was fearful. Four men together wanted her.

She couldn't think another coherent thought as Brody deepened the kiss and pulled her into his arms.

She kissed him back, and when his hand moved under her dress to her ass, squeezing the cheek, she moaned.

Then came the thought that someone might walk in. They were right inside the damn kitchen. He must have sensed her pulling away because he slowly released her lips.

He pulled back, taking her hand firmly within his much larger one. "Come with me."

She only hesitated a moment, but one tug on her hand and she followed, her desire to taste more of this exquisite, complicated man leading her along the way.

They cut through the backyard, away from the party and all the people. He escorted her to a larger building she had seen before but had no idea what was in it. At the door, he pressed her hard against the siding and kissed her again. It seemed that neither of them could get enough of one another, and as he continued to kiss her while pulling the door open, she hadn't a care in the world.

Somehow, Brody got her inside the dark building and closed then locked the door. He pressed her against it, kissing her deeply while exploring her body with his hands.

He moved his hands to her panties as he released her lips.

The light was dull inside of the building. She could barely make out what was around them but really didn't care. Brody's hard, thick fingers pressed against her mound and she gasped, grabbing his wrist.

"Brody?"

"Open for me, Amelia. Let me be the first one to make you come, baby. The first one to stroke this wet pussy and start learning this perfect body."

She held his intense gaze and felt the slight twinge of fear caused by his size, his personality, and of course, her resistance to giving herself in fear of getting her heart broken. Then she thought about Mano. The man had put a deeper fear in her than she thought.

He kissed her softly, pressing fingers to her pussy lips while his other hand pressed against her hip and the wall. He was in total control and she would be lying if she said she wasn't turned on by this.

"Brody, I'm scared." She held his wrist and the urge to let him touch her and ease the ache building inside of her nearly overpowered the fear.

He stopped touching her then pulled her into his arms. He lifted her up. She straddled his waist, feeling his belt buckle and thick waist wedge against her inner thighs. Her pussy wept and her nipples instantly hardened.

"Don't be afraid of me. I care about you. I want to get to know you. I want to touch, lick, and suck every inch of this body. I want you to look at me and care."

She held his shoulders and felt the muscles beneath her palms. The tears welled up in her eyes as she lowered her eyes to his chest. The first two buttons were undone. She could see his tan skin and imagined pressing her fingers inside the material and feeling his heart beat. Would it be racing, just like hers was right now?

"Amelia? Amelia, look at me." She shook her head. She feared that the tears may fall. She feared being weak after fighting to be strong for so long.

Brody lowered her feet to the ground and pressed her against the wall using his hips to hold her in place before cupping her face between his hands.

She looked into his eyes and her heart raced.

"You're shaking. Do I really scare you?" he whispered.

She shook her head. She feared taking a chance on him and his brothers. She feared the past, especially after Mano's voice message today.

"I'm so sorry, Brody. I thought. I mean, I really like you. It's just that maybe I thought I was ready, but I'm not. I'm scared, Brody."

He brushed his thumb along her lower lip.

"Afraid of what?"

She swallowed hard. "Of feeling…anything."

His expression grew dark and almost angry.

"Who hurt you? Tell me." She was shocked by his evaluation. She shouldn't deny it. She couldn't lie to him.

"It doesn't matter. *He* doesn't matter."

"Obviously the asshole does matter because he's standing between all of us and what could possibly be perfect. He hurt you, and I want to know about it."

"No, Brody." She shook her head and pulled away. He released her and she took a few unsteady steps, but then he grabbed her hand. When he pulled her back, he wrapped his arms around her from behind and laid his head on her shoulder.

"My brothers and I would never hurt you. We know far too well about pain, Amelia. I've been hurting for so long, I didn't think I had a heart."

"Oh, Brody, this has nothing to do with you."

He squeezed her harder and she leaned back as he placed his cheek against hers. "You're wrong. It is about me. It's about us and about the others. We've all been hurt, baby. We've all had our share of heartache and sadness. Some of us have had it longer, that's all."

She took a deep breath and released it.

"You're not shaking so much now." He turned his cheek so he could kiss her skin.

"It feels good in your arms. You're so big and strong and it makes me feel safe."

He adjusted his stance and she felt his long, hard erection slide up her lower back and ass. "That's good, because you are safe in these arms. I could hold you like this forever." He started kissing her more and when his lips touched hers, she turned in his arms and kissed him back.

Their exploration became more urgent. Somehow her hands managed to move under his shirt and she rubbed her palms along his taut muscles and nipples. He maneuvered his hand under her dress and down her panties.

The moment his fingers touched her cunt, Amelia moaned into Brody's mouth. There was no stopping them. All she wanted to do was feel. So Amelia ran her hands up and down his chest as he pressed his thighs between her legs, moved her against the wall, and pressed two fingers up into her pussy.

He released her lips and began kissing her neck as he stoked her pussy.

"Oh God, Brody." She moaned and he licked her skin and continued to tease her cunt, and draw out more of her cream with every stroke of his fingers.

She felt her body tighten up, and she gripped his arms, tilted her head back, and moaned her release.

"Beautiful." He covered her mouth and kissed her until she came down from the effects of an incredible orgasm.

* * * *

Brody pulled Amelia into his arms and hugged her to him. He inhaled the sweet smell of her shampoo and absorbed the feel of her body against him.

"Are you okay?" he asked, and she nodded her head against his chest. "Thank you for trusting me with that."

She looked up at him and he could see the blush against her cheeks and the sparkle in her eyes. "You're thanking me? I think I should be thanking you. That was…amazing, Brody."

He felt the smile nearly reach his lips. It had been so long since he smiled or even felt like it.

He smoothed out her dress and she adjusted her breasts in the snug-fitting material.

"You have an amazing body. I can't wait to explore every inch of it." He moved the palm of his hand over her ass. He wanted to be inside of her so badly his cock was throbbing for release.

"Brody, this was a huge step for me. I'm not—"

He placed his finger over her lips. He didn't want to hear her denials or her attempts at putting the damn imaginary wall back up.

"No, baby, don't say anymore. Let's just enjoy this, okay? Do you want to head back to the party?"

"I'm not sure I can walk."

He laughed then scooped her up into his arms. Amelia squealed but wrapped her arms around his neck and snuggled close.

"I'll carry you."

"Won't that draw attention to us?"

"If it sends a message that you belong to me, then I'm all for it."

"Brody, will the others be upset?"

He knew she was attracted to him and his brothers. She could deny it and fight these feelings all she wanted.

He shook his head. "No, Amelia. They'll be really happy."

"Are you certain?"

"They'll want what I just had. To see your angelic face blush with satisfaction as they get to watch you come. You're beautiful."

She leaned forward and kissed him. "I think you need to put me down. I'm not quite ready to be made a spectacle of. I have a lot to think about in regards to a relationship like this."

He slowly set her down. "I'm glad to hear that you'll consider us. But you're not getting off easy." He grabbed her hand and brought her fingers to his lips and kissed them. "Let's get back to the party."

He held her hand and there was no way he was letting her go.

* * * *

Amelia was laughing at something Regan was saying. Regan could be so dramatic when telling a story. Her facial expressions alone, were funny.

Amelia felt the hand on her waist, but it was the second hand on her knee, caressing back and forth that was causing her anxiety. Well, maybe anxiety was the wrong word.

Brody sat beside her on the stool by the outside bar. His arm was around her waist, keeping her close. Her legs were crossed as she listened to Regan speaking and the different conversations that flowed from one subject to another. She felt lost in the fun, uplifting atmosphere. Then Murphy sat beside her. He immediately placed his hand on her knee and began to caress it.

The instant sting of what she could only describe as fire lit up her entire body. An imaginary line from his touch, combined with Brody's, seemed to connect to her pussy. Her belly tightened, her breasts felt full and aroused, and she actually felt the hitch in her breath.

One glance around them, and she noticed the eyes on her. These men were making a scene. They were staking a claim, a public move, and Amelia had mixed emotions.

She could feel her body began to shake as she went to clasp her hands only for them to hit Murphy's large one. She stared down at his hand. It was huge, muscular, his fingers thick and long. She wasn't certain why she imagined his cock in her mind. It came on instant, nearly making her gasp.

She felt Brody's thumb caress her hip bone. Even though the clothing covered her skin, it felt obsolete. His simple, gentle touch was that powerful.

Her mind traveled in all sorts of directions, and as the other people around them went about a conversation she couldn't follow if she tried, Murphy moved closer. As he leaned into her, she felt the palm of his hand glide up her thigh and to the seat bottom where her thigh and ass connected with the wood.

"I want to be alone with you. So do my brothers."

She looked at him. The tone of his deep voice penetrated through her skin. As she took a slow breath, it hitched in her throat and her voice cracked as she answered him.

"Murphy, I'm not sure about this."

She felt his hand squeeze her upper thigh under her dress, and she pressed her hand down, feeling completely exposed from his move. A quick look around her and she noticed the crowd disperse into separate little group conversations as Ricky and Waylon pulled over two more stools. The scraping of the chair legs announced to all that chairs were moving hard, across the wooden planked floors.

She looked up to see Regan squint. Then a huge smiled crossed her face. Ricky's and Waylon's knees tapped against hers as they sat down on the stools they moved.

She swallowed hard. These men were so large. Not just in size, but in personality and persona. When one entered a room, all noticed. Now, as four moved to surround little ole her, the atmosphere changed instantly.

Murphy squeezed her thigh again in an attempt to make her focus on him. Waylon and Murphy spoke as Ricky leaned forward and squeezed her knee.

"We're going to sit here for a few more minutes and that's all. Then we're going to say good night, we're going to walk you to your cottage, and you're going to ask us inside," Murphy whispered.

She was about to respond when Brody squeezed her hip to get her attention. She turned toward him.

"Then you can decide what happens next. But be warned, watching you all day talking, laughing, enjoying spending time with our family and friends has been torture for me and for my brothers. We want you to ourselves." He leaned in, her head absorbed his words, and then he kissed her softly on the lips. As Murphy squeezed and caressed her, she nearly shot off the chair. Her pussy wept in excitement and arousal. Two men were touching her at once and she liked it. She wanted more of it. Immediately she pulled from Brody. She looked at Ricky, a smile on his face. The hunger in his eyes held her gaze. Then Waylon sat back. His big muscular arms were crossed in front of his chest and his expression was firm, like stone.

The chairs scraped against the wood again, as Ricky and Brody stood up. The moment Brody moved his hand off of her waist she felt the loss of his touch.

Murphy smoothed his hand slowly from her thigh and stood up next.

Brody offered his hand.

"Wait," she said, sliding off the stool. She looked around in a panic, but no one was watching them. The others were laughing and enjoying the music. It was dark outside now as Waylon and Ricky walked off the porch and into the darkness.

Murphy gave her a very stern look. "Don't keep us waiting." Those words ran havoc on her insides.

"I have to grab my purse and say good night."

"Make it fast," Brody said then turned her around and wrapped an arm around her waist. She gasped at his quick move and felt the twinge of excitement arouse her body in all the right places.

He kissed her neck, her shoulder then cheek. "Don't be scared. We'll go as slow as you need, but to be completely honest, Amelia, as I feel you in my arms, going slow is the last thing I want to do with you."

Before she could speak, he was escorting her around the porch to say good-bye and then into the kitchen, where his dads and mom were talking. They each gave her a hug and said good night.

Brody grabbed her purse for her as his mom made certain that Amelia wasn't driving back to the cottage alone.

Brody ensured her that he would escort her home because she had work tomorrow morning.

She wondered if his parents knew him and his brothers' intentions? They didn't seem to indicate a disapproval of their obvious attraction, so that made Amelia feel less self-conscious. It was odd to have that sensation. The Haases weren't her parents, yet here she was acting like they might be disappointed in her behavior. When had she become desperate for parents or a family of her own? Had spending a mere three weeks in Houston made her envious of Regan's life and family? Had it really been only three weeks since arriving here and working? It seemed so much longer, yet here she was, ready to expose her heart to four men in a type of relationship she really didn't understand.

She exited the house with Brody holding her hand.

"Do you have your keys?" he asked.

She nodded and reached into her purse to grab them. As she took them out, he turned her around, taking the keys from her hand before pulling her close. He leaned down and kissed her deeply.

Brody, known as Ice, was anything but cold in the way he kissed her. She was instantly lost in his kiss and even in the possessive way he moved his hands over her body, up under her hair, gripping the locks and directing her head as he devoured her moans. When he finally had his fill, he turned her around, opened the passenger door, and helped her into the seat.

She was in shock. She felt so damn horny despite her fear of knowing that three other big, sexy men waited for them at her cottage. Men that wanted to touch her, kiss her, and perhaps have sex with her.

She felt that nervous, achy feeling in her gut as she clasped her hands together. As Brody drove up the driveway and onto the stone path, far from any other people and secluded from interruption, she gulped.

Brody parked her car, turned off the lights and ignition, then got out. Before she could move or perhaps take a second to breathe, overthink this, or panic, her door opened and Murphy was there, reaching a hand toward her.

She gripped her purse then placed her hand into his. As he pulled her up and against him, he covered her mouth with his own.

* * * *

Murphy was desperate to taste her, to take off her pretty little dress and explore her sexy body.

He couldn't help the feelings of desperation he had as he continued to kiss her deeply. When she wrapped her arms around his neck in compliance, he rejoiced inside as he lifted her up and against him.

Her thighs wrapped around his waist as he cupped her ass under her dress and felt the bare skin then the tight material against the crack. Her and the damn thong panties drove him wild. His dick was so fucking hard as he walked effortlessly with her in his arms.

They reached the doorway his brothers held open and went inside. She dropped her purse. He heard it hit the floor as he carried her straight to the bedroom.

Once inside he lowered her to the bed and was pressed between her open thighs. Releasing her lips and panting for breath, he stared down into her dark brown eyes and was lost in emotion.

"Please invite us to stay. Don't think, don't fear, just follow your heart, Amelia."

She stared at him and then his brothers as they entered her small bedroom.

"I think I lost my mind," she whispered and he smiled.

"Baby, we're feeling the exact same way. Let us love you tonight."

Murphy leaned down and lifted her dress up, revealing dark lace panties and her firm belly. He noticed the tattoo as he leaned his lips closer, licking across her skin. She pushed her pelvis up toward him and he smiled.

"I need to taste you, baby." He reached for her panties. He maneuvered his fingers under the thin material and slowly pulled her panties down her sexy body. Her feminine scent aroused something carnal inside of Murphy. As he moved his hands up her thighs and heard his brothers begin to undress, he realized just how feminine and small in size she was to them. With palms spreading her toned thighs wider, he could practically cover her thigh completely.

"You smell so good, Amelia. So fucking good."

He licked across her sweet folds and felt her shiver. She tried to close her thighs.

"Stay open for him, for us." Waylon's authoritative voice penetrated the air and made Amelia freeze. Murphy felt her tense until he licked across her pussy lips again. She moaned then eased her ass down deeper against the comforter.

Using his thumbs to spread those delicious lips, he stroked her gently.

"You have the prettiest little pussy, baby. All trim and neat." He pressed a digit up into her and she grabbed his wrist.

"Murphy." She said his name and his dick somehow grew harder.

"Fuck, baby, I love it when you say my name."

"Let go of his wrist, Amelia," Brody stated then knelt down onto the bed. He was naked, holding his dick in his hand, and Amelia gasped.

"Oh God, Brody. Oh my God, this is too much. You guys are too much."

"Not too much. We're all meant for this, for you," Ricky said.

Murphy added a second digit to her pussy and began to move in and out of her. With every stroke she tilted upward, causing her breasts to push upward, too. Ricky helped remove her dress. She wiggled her ass at him and Brody assisted with getting the material over her head. All she wore now was a strapless black bra that joined her large breasts together causing a deep cleavage.

Ricky and Brody reached for the clasp next and removed the last bit of clothing that covered their goddess.

"Fuck, baby, you're fucking hot." Ricky cupped her breast. Brody cupped her other breast then leaned down and licked the tip.

The sight was so erotic and powerful, Murphy was shocked at how turned on he felt. He and his brothers were close. They never shared a woman before but knew that they wanted to. Amelia was special.

"Give me your hands," Waylon stated then took Amelia's hands and raised them above her head. He kissed her palms then her forearms and finally her mouth. She tilted her head back toward him, because he was behind her. She was stretched out before them. Murphy knew he needed to get inside of her or he would lose it right here.

"Amelia, baby, I want you, honey. I want to make love to you, sweetheart," Murphy said then stood up. Brody and Ricky caressed her inner thighs open as Waylon released her lips then caressed his palms down her breast and to her pussy. Murphy undressed quickly.

"Are you on the pill, baby?"

"Yes," she whispered.

* * * *

Amelia felt desperate. She craved more of them. She felt incredibly turned on and ready to engage in this.

As Waylon hovered over her from behind her head, she felt his thick cock against her cheek as his hands caressed her breasts. When he trailed a finger over her pussy and pressed it between her wet folds, she tried to close her legs as an instant flow of cream released. Brody and Ricky wouldn't allow it. Their large, wide hands held her open. "Oh." She moaned and something carnal and wild came over her. She turned to the side and licked along Waylon's cock.

"Fuck, baby, do that again," Waylon said and so she did. He eased back and moved her slightly so that she could taste him. Simultaneously she felt Murphy move between her legs and heard Ricky and Brody make comments about how hot and sexy she looked. She pulled Waylon's cock between her lips and sucked as much of him as she could. He gripped her hair and she moaned against his cock.

"Son of a bitch, Amelia. You're going to make me come, baby." Waylon eased his cock in and out of her mouth.

"Damn, woman, you've got me there already," Murphy said then pushed his cock into her pussy.

She gasped at his size and girth, releasing Waylon's cock from her mouth.

Ricky and Brody grabbed her hands and held them above her head. She was at their will and mercy as she exploded and shook with her first orgasm.

"Gorgeous. You look incredible when you come," Murphy said then increased his thrusts. He stroked his cock against her pussy then pulled back and thrust into her deeply. She moaned a little louder as the others released her and Murphy grabbed a hold of her hands. They locked gazes and Amelia smiled. Murphy looked so intense and controlled.

He leaned down and kissed her hard on the mouth. She wrapped her arms around his shoulders and kissed him back. They were trying to battle over control of the kiss, and with every stroke of Murphy's cock she allowed him to take over. Soon he was pulling from her mouth and kissing along her neck as he thrust into her. Amelia reached around and tried to grab his ass. She ran her hands along the muscles of his hips and back, and she spread her legs wider.

Tilting her head back, she felt him grow thicker and knew he was going to come.

"Come with me, Amelia," he ordered. She called out his name as she exploded, and he followed suit before cradling her in his arms and rolling to his side. She lay against Murphy, calming her breathing and kissing his chest. His hands caressed over her ass and hip then up over the sides of her breast, tickling her.

"Murphy." She reprimanded then tried to get up. He held her tight and she knew in his grasp and embrace she couldn't get up unless he allowed it. Murphy had to be in control at all times.

When she felt the second set of hands on her, caressing her thigh then rolling her away from Murphy, she waited to see if they would argue or fight. Instead Murphy winked at her then stood up from the bed. She turned toward Ricky. He smiled down at her then scooted between her legs.

Rubbing the palms of his hands together, he stared at her breasts and pussy as he licked his lips.

"So, where do I start?" he teased and she giggled. Ricky had a hell of a body on him and tattoos along his arm and shoulder. She noticed the scars on his chest immediately. He shook his head at her. "No worries. Just battle wounds."

She swallowed hard.

She stared at him in awe. These men had perfect physiques.

He cupped her breasts first, and she softly moaned and closed her eyes. "Look at me."

She immediately did as Ricky said. Her eyes were wide and she probably appeared fearful because he smiled then winked.

"You're going to learn soon enough, that my brothers and I like to be in control in the bedroom."

"And everywhere else," Waylon added, and they all chuckled. The sound of four masculine chuckles made her pussy leak. She was so horny right now everything about them turned her on.

She moved her hands up to his waist as he leaned down and licked across her nipple. Ricky took his time kissing, licking, and sucking each breast, and Amelia found herself lost in his caresses as she tilted her pussy up against him.

"Ricky, please."

"What do you need, baby?" he asked her as he suckled against her neck and shoulder, making her squirm beneath him.

"You," she said and he chuckled.

"I'm right here."

He eased his way inside of her, slowly pressing his cock into her cunt. With each inch she moaned and opened wider for him. She felt so needy and as if the only thing that could ease the ache inside was Ricky's cock.

"That's it, baby. God, Amelia, you feel so tight."

He thrust all the way in then sat up pulling her legs up over his thighs.

"Ricky," she reprimanded.

"I've dreamed about this moment." He began a series of long, deep thrusts into her pussy.

He grabbed her wrists, placed them above her head as he leaned down over her, and thrust his hips, rotating them, pulling out then thrusting back in with deep, penetrating caresses.

"Perfection." He covered her mouth and kissed her.

Soon, he released her wrists and began to make love to her faster. His strokes were relentless as she ran her fingers through his hair and counterthrust up against him. Her body tightened like a bow then snapped as she called his name. Ricky continued to thrust into her three more times then exploded inside of her. He wrapped her in his arms, crushing her momentarily to the bed before he rolled to his side taking her with him.

She hugged him tight as he caressed her lower back then her ass and trailed a finger down the crack.

"You have a great ass, Amelia. I can't wait to fuck it."

She sat up, completely caught off guard by his statement. They all chuckled.

"Don't scare her, Ricky. She's new to this," Brody said, then lifted her up and pulled her on top of him. Ricky rolled over and got up off the bed.

The light in the room was dim, but she could see some scars on Brody's chiseled chest. They were sporadic, and appeared like knife marks.

Amelia straddled Brody's hips, feeling his long thick cock under her ass and pussy. She couldn't help the mix of emotions she felt. She was instantly concerned and wondered how he sustained his injuries. She then panicked and hoped that he and his brothers wouldn't notice hers, in this dim light.

Brody thrust his cock upward.

She closed her eyes and turned away from him in embarrassment. Meanwhile, she'd just had sex with his brothers and certainly was going to have sex with Brody and Waylon next.

Brody grabbed a hold of her hips and thrust upward again. "Look at me."

She shyly looked down. The feel of his large hands moving softly up her hips to cup both breasts aroused her senses. She felt her pussy leak then jerked when Brody pinched both nipples.

He eased the pinch he caused by rolling the pink protruding flesh between two fingers. He somehow used his thumbs to caress the mounds at the same time, and Amelia began to slowly move on him.

"Take me inside of you, Amelia. Make me come, like I made you come in the barn tonight."

She was embarrassed a moment then felt the hands smooth along her shoulders. Waylon was behind her, caressing her skin.

He reached her hips and thighs, caressing them, sending tingling sensations underneath her skin.

"Lift up, baby, and take Brody's cock, while I explore this ass of yours." He lifted her, and Brody aligned his cock with her pussy, as she adjusted her hips with Waylon's guidance. Then she lowered onto Brody's cock.

"That's it, baby. Nice and easy." Brody held her hips, and she slowly adjusted to his girth.

Up and down, too slow apparently for Brody, because he ground his teeth and nearly growled while she rode him.

Meanwhile, the feel of Waylon's hands caressing her ass cheeks, parting them, then stroking her anus had her moving faster.

"Whatever you're doing Waylon, she likes it. Keep it up," Brody said then thrust hard upward, causing Amelia to grab onto his shoulders and fall forward.

As she gasped in shock at Brody's strength and power, she felt a finger press to her forbidden hole just as she lowered onto Brody's cock again.

"Oh God, it burns," she stated aloud. Brody held her in place then lifted her up and pulled her back down onto his shaft hard. She was overwhelmed with fullness and need.

She pushed her ass back against Waylon's fingers.

"Ride them, Amelia. Do it," Murphy commanded. She closed her eyes as Brody roared and thrust up and down as he held her hips so tight. Now her chest was flat against Brody's as he thrust upward while Waylon finger-fucked her ass.

She screamed as the orgasm overtook her, but she continued to thrust back against Waylon then downward against Brody.

Brody roared his release, but before she could catch her breath, Waylon wrapped an arm around her waist to hoist her off of Brody. He pulled her to the edge, parted her thighs, and thrust into her to the hilt. She screamed from his invasion, so turned on by his power trip she gasped for air. His arm, like a vise grip around her waist as he held himself deep inside her pussy, kept her steady on all fours.

He pushed her hair from her face.

"You are so fucking perfect. I can't go slow, Amelia. I don't think I ever will be able to with you."

She felt his words to her heart and soul. Her core urged him to thrust into her, to fuck her hard, and as she began to say the words, Waylon pulled out then thrust back in. She gripped the comforter and felt her breasts sway with every deep thrust of his cock into her.

"You belong to us now, Amelia. No more flirting. No one else but us." He thrust again and again.

"Say it," he demanded but she couldn't speak.

He smacked her ass and she screamed a small release.

"Say it."

"You. Just the four of you." She cried out as her body shook and convulsed from the hardest orgasm yet.

Waylon pulled out and shoved back in, in a series of long, hard, fast thrusts. She could hardly remain upward and felt her legs shaking.

"Ours," he stated loudly then thrust into her deeply, wrapping her in his arm as she lost the ability to remain upright and collapsed to the bed. Waylon landed on top of her but somehow managed to keep most of his weight off of her.

He pulled her backward so that her back lay flat against his chest while his arm remained wrapped around her midsection cupping a breast and stroking her nipple between two fingers. She opened her eyes to see Murphy standing there smiling.

"You look lovely, Amelia."

"Tired." She felt herself drifting off into sleep and in the warmth of Waylon's arms, with her lovers all around her.

Chapter 9

Amelia awoke to the sound of her alarm going off. Instantly she felt the hand cupping her breast and the hard body behind her. Someone walked into the room and turned off the alarm.

"Good morning."

She peeked her eye open and saw Ricky standing there holding a hot cup of coffee and smiling.

Waylon pressed his lips against her shoulder as he gave her breast a squeeze.

"Morning," she said, and as she moved, she felt the soreness and made a noise.

Immediately Ricky's smile turned to a frown and Waylon uncupped her breast and sat up.

"Are you okay?" they asked.

She closed her eyes and adjusted her body. She pulled the sheets up against her chest and cringed. "I'm good."

Waylon pulled her gently back down onto the bed and placed his arm over her waist. He looked her over then stared into her eyes with such serious concern she nearly lost the ability to breathe. Tears stung her eyes at his show of care and affection. Could last night have meant more than just really good sex? She realized instantly that she hoped so.

"I'm okay, just a little sore."

"Did we hurt you?" Ricky asked.

She shook her head.

"What's going on?" Brody asked as he and Murphy entered the room. She caught sight of them with their bare chests and only wearing jeans.

She licked her bottom lip. Waylon pressed his hand against her cheek and chin then held her firmly as he stared down into her eyes.

"Amelia, are you sure we didn't hurt you."

"Yes. It's just been a while for me, okay, Waylon? I need to get up and shower. I can't be late for work."

He leaned down and kissed her softly on the lips.

He looked at her when he released her lips, as if she weren't telling the truth. Apparently she wasn't the only one in this room with trust issues.

Ricky helped her get up from the bed and the sheets fell away from her body.

He moved the palm of his hand along her side then pulled her against his chest. She hugged him, loving the feel of being in his arms. She could get lost in such big strong arms like Ricky's.

When he moved his hand over her ass and squeezed, she felt her body react. If she didn't get into the shower now, she may be playing hookie for the very first time in her life.

"I have to get ready," she whispered.

He released her, and as she looked over her shoulder, four sets of eyes remained glued on her body. She smiled, feeling confident and sexy as she made her way into the small bathroom.

* * * *

They were making breakfast when Waylon heard Amelia's phone ringing.

"That thing's been going off all morning," Murphy stated.

Waylon reached inside and pulled out the cell phone. He missed the call, but noticed that there were several text messages.

He hit the screen.

"What are you doing, Waylon?" Murphy asked.

"Seeing who's calling her."

"Don't," Ricky told him.

He looked at his brothers. "I want to know who's calling her. We don't know anything about her life in New York or who that guy was in the picture the day she moved in here."

"Whoever he was, he hurt her. She was scared for me to touch her. I told you about that last night," Brody stated.

Waylon put the phone back down.

He ran his hand through his crew cut hair.

"You're right. I'm fucking not used to this. I don't want her out of my sight. I don't know how to handle this."

"Calm down, Waylon. We're all feeling the same way," Ricky stated.

"Yeah, you don't think I thought of turning that alarm clock off so she would oversleep, just so there was more time with her in bed?" Murphy asked.

Ricky chuckled.

"Last night, this morning…this is more than I ever imagined it would be like," Brody told them.

Waylon felt his chest tighten. He didn't do emotions well. In fact, he ran from his own. "I don't want to leave for Vegas Friday."

His brothers were quiet.

"This is a lot to take in. We need to slow things down and not act so possessive. It could scare Amelia," Ricky said.

"Do we agree to take our time here? Maybe let her get to know us individually, too?" Brody asked.

"Agreed," Murphy replied. Then Ricky followed and Waylon was last.

He knew this was going to be difficult for him. All these years home and he avoided getting down to his fears and emotions. One passionate night with Amelia, and a whole new light had been shed upon his life and his attitude.

He couldn't lose her. She was instantly so important, and he would do what was necessary to hold on to her forever.

Chapter 10

Amelia finished setting up the display tables in the hospital. She gathered all the brochures about the programs and put out some nice baked goods for the two volunteers that would run the table.

She felt her cell phone vibrating against her hip and fear gripped her insides.

Mano had called her three times last night and texted, too. When she walked out into the kitchen this morning, she saw her phone on the counter and prayed that none of the men had seen it. They could misinterpret Mano's words as something of meaning to her. Mano was a pig.

His words and his text messages showed his arrogance. As she checked out the caller ID, she didn't recognize the number. Amelia debated about answering it as she headed toward the atrium doors. She would have privacy out there.

"Hello."

"I was going to pretend that you never received my first message, but the other five? Come on, Amelia. You can't still be angry with me," Mano stated.

Her blood pressure rose beyond the fear of his wrath.

"Angry with you still? What the hell do you think, Mano? Of course I am. Disappearing for a year didn't send a clear and precise message?" She looked around her, grateful that no one was there to hear her raise her voice.

"I know I fucked up. Hell, Amelia, I was caught up in feeling like I wasn't good enough. I drank too much that night. Those women meant nothing."

"Stop! Just stop it right now. I can't believe you, Mano. It's been over a year. What about Kyle? Explain that one, Mano. If you cared, then why hadn't you stopped that fight?"

"Your brother made the decision to get in the ring with that monster."

"You had money on it. You know what? I'm not interested in anything that you have to say. It's always about you. It didn't work out. It's over. I meant nothing and I got it loud and clear."

"Don't hang up, Amelia. Let me explain. Let me apologize. When I heard that you were in the city, I fucking rushed there from across town. You were gone before I had the chance to tell you in person."

"To tell me what?"

"That I'm making it big now. No small time anymore. No underground, illegal shit."

"You don't seem to get it, Mano. I don't care. That life is behind me. You're behind me. I've moved on. I need to go."

"I'm not behind you. We're meant to be. What, did you fucking say that you moved on? Are you fucking some other guy?"

"Stop it. It's been over since the moment I caught you in bed with those two whores and the second you beat me and blamed me for all your faults."

"You are fucking someone else. Who the fuck is he? I want to know right now 'cause he's a fucking dead man walking!"

"Don't call me ever again."

"Oh I will and I might even take a trip out to Houston to see you in person."

She disconnected the call.

She was so angry. Hearing his voice brought back so many bad memories and feelings. She didn't need this shit right now when she had so much to worry about with Murphy, Ricky, Waylon, and Brody.

She'd thought about them all day today. She was starting to have second thoughts about last night. Not total regret. No way. Not with men so sexy and charismatic as the four of them. They each represented things she was afraid of and had yet to overcome. She would have to take things slow. Murphy's commanding, bossy attitude worried her. He was a big man. When he said jump, he expected instant response. Ricky, well Ricky was a character. He was a flirt and she feared he could stray. But those scars on his chest said a lot. Maybe he was like her? Maybe he acted so confident and showed face to keep his true insecurities at bay?

But she still feared that any of them could turn on her as Mano had. After all, Mano claimed to have loved her and thought her his world, and then she busted him in bed with those two women. She felt her chest tighten. She thought about Brody. A soldier, cold as ice, serious as could be. He reminded her of the fear she had losing her father and brothers to the scars of war. Not only physical, but also emotional. Would he let her in? Could she let him in and share the abuse she sustained with Mano? How about her own scars? Both were hidden, and the one against her hip that the tattoo hid. They would see it. They would notice the raised skin and ask questions. She would fear that moment of truth. Then there was Waylon. Waylon, she feared most of all. He, too, was a soldier, scarred by his experiences, which explained his seriousness and demanding personality. He used his fists as a profession and it of course reminded her of Mano and of her brother, Kyle. Kyle refused to receive counseling or at minimum talk to her about his feelings. His rage showed in the ring. It showed when he did drugs and when he tossed her across the room like a rag doll.

That could be Waylon. Not that she knew much about him, except for what Regan explained, but the fear was still there. He'd spanked her ass while they were having sex. That had ultimately turned her on, but now she wondered if his show of dominance was an early sign of physical abuse.

That thought brought tears to her eyes and an instant pain in her chest.

Amelia turned around and headed back to the table. The volunteers were arriving and she needed to get them all set up then head back upstairs to the office.

As she turned the corner, she saw Tucker. He was talking to a couple of the men in the group that were headed to a meeting upstairs. She turned around and was ready to take the stairs when she heard her name being called.

"Amelia! Come on, we'll hold it for you," one of the guy's, Billy, yelled. The others smiled, but Tucker looked smug.

"You work here?" he asked and she nodded her head.

"She's new. But a favorite already," Billy whispered then gave her a wink.

"Thanks."

"What do you do?" Tucker asked and she didn't want to talk to him or be polite. The guy had been a jerk.

"She works for your dad, Tucker," Johnny stated.

"No shit. Damn, if I knew that, I would stop in here more often," Tucker said flirtatiously. The others chuckled.

As the doors opened, Amelia stepped out first.

Toby was there to greet her and Tucker.

"Hey, you two came up together?" he asked as the other guys waved then headed down to the meeting room.

"Yeah, I didn't know Amelia worked for you."

"Sure does, son. She's beautiful, right?"

"And then some," Tucker replied and Toby chuckled.

"Oh, Amelia, Murphy Haas called for you. He left his cell number."

She smiled. "Great. Thank you. Listen, I have everything set up downstairs. The volunteers have arrived. In an hour or so, I'll go down to check on them."

"Okay. Great. I need to run down the hall. Tucker, you know where the envelope on my desk is. I'll be back in a few minutes." Was it Amelia, or did Toby seem annoyed with his son? She got a feeling that Tucker's visit was not appreciated. But maybe she was wrong. All she knew was that Tucker was a jerk that night at the bar.

"No problem. I'll keep Amelia company," Tucker said, but Toby was already out the door and hadn't heard his son.

Amelia ignored Tucker's flirtatious comment and walked to the small desk. She peeled the sticky note from the screen on her computer. It had Murphy's name and cell phone number on it. As she looked up, she noticed Tucker, holding an envelope and leaning against the door frame, staring at her.

She walked around her desk to the file cabinet and began to look up some information she needed for the last group of the day.

"Not calling back your bodyguard?"

She turned to look at him. "Excuse me?"

He stepped away from the doorway as she grabbed the paper she needed then walked over to the photocopying machine.

She knew that Tucker approached. Every nerve in her body alerted her to not let her guard down.

When she felt his finger glide down her spine, she turned around.

"Don't touch me."

He held her gaze as he stared into her eyes. "You fucking him?"

She couldn't believe his nerve. "Get out of here."

"You know that him and his brothers share? They pick up women all the time, bring them back to their house and pretend they never shared before."

She felt her heart sink. He was lying. He was an asshole and was working to get a rile out of her. He was doing a great job.

"You need to leave."

He shook his head then made a noise with his tongue as he reached out to twirl a piece of hair between his fingers.

"I'm watching you. And that cute little sister of Regan's."

"You stay away from her. I swear Tucker. Stay clear of Regan and her sister."

He raised his one eyebrow at her and it gave her the creeps.

"Jealous?"

She gave him a dirty look. She knew he was trying to rattle her. His eyes zeroed in on her breasts and then her lips.

"I never got to kiss you that night. After letting me feel your ass on the dance floor, you could have at least let me get a little."

"I didn't let you do any such thing. Get out of here."

He reached out and ran his finger over her lip. She shoved his hand away, and a very determined, angry expression reached his eyes. This guy was no good. He was dangerous and her gut clenched as it identified the signals.

"See ya around, darling."

He started to head out, and as he turned, his father Toby was coming back.

"Hey, you're still here? I'll walk you out. I really don't need this today."

She watched Toby's expression change to annoyance, but Tucker hadn't taken his eyes off of Amelia.

"See ya around, Amelia."

Toby smiled toward her. "I'll be back in ten."

Amelia watched Tucker walk away with his father. What an asshole. She'd have to warn Regan and Velma.

She heard the phone ring at her desk and answered it.

"Hey, I thought I'd hear back from you by now. Busy day?" Murphy asked.

She was still on edge from Tucker.

"Give me some breathing room, Murphy. I just got your message like ten minutes ago," she snapped and felt bad as she slapped her hand to her forehead. This was Murphy she was barking at. He would not like that.

"What's wrong?" he asked. How the hell can he know something is wrong?

She took a deep breath and released it. "Long story. It doesn't matter. I'm sorry to have barked at you. I'm glad you called."

"You are?"

"Yes. I think we need to talk."

"Uh-oh. That doesn't sound good, darling. What's the matter?"

She took a deep breath than released it. "Now isn't the time. I leave in a couple of hours. How about I call you when I get home, after I shower?"

"Maybe some company in that shower might help?"

She felt her belly tighten and her pussy actually reacted in sync to his words. *Damn, I have it bad.*

"Please, Murphy. I need things to go slow."

"What happened today, to make you overthink things and regret last night?"

"I didn't say I regretted last night. I definitely don't regret it."

"Good. So spit it out."

"Murphy, stop. I'll talk to you later. I need to go."

"We'll be waiting there for you. Prepare to spill the beans."

* * * *

"So what do you think is up, Murphy?" Ricky asked as he leaned against his truck outside of Amelia's cottage. She should have been home an hour ago. Waylon and Brody were leaning against the SUV.

"Not sure. Maybe just cold feet. This type of relationship is new to her," Murphy stated.

"It's new to us, too," Waylon replied with an attitude. He kept looking toward the roadway. Murphy was beginning to realize how untrusting they were.

They heard Amelia's loud car make its way up the driveway. She pulled into the spot near the house and turned off the engine. It made a funny noise that Murphy didn't like.

One look at Brody, and he could tell that his brother was thinking the same thing.

Amelia stepped out of the car. Her thigh-length skirt tapped against her legs as he absorbed her from high heels to sleeveless blouse. This morning, when she emerged from the bedroom, his heart nearly skipped a beat. Their woman was a knockout.

"You're late," Waylon said from behind him as Murphy held her door open. She looked tired.

"I told Murphy that I would call once I got home. I needed to go to the store. I forgot to take something out for dinner."

"That's no problem, darling. We'll help you out," Ricky stated. She walked to the back of the car and opened up the trunk. They each carried in a bag then closed the trunk and followed Amelia to the front door.

He watched as she began unpacking the bags and placing things into the refrigerator and the cabinets.

"So, what was it that you wanted to talk about?" Ricky asked as Amelia placed the last item into the cabinet. She turned around to face them.

"I need things to go slowly. I don't know hardly anything about any of you and well, I don't make it a habit to sleep around. Perhaps you guys do, or you're used to this type of relationship, but I'm not. I'm nervous and I'm worried and—"

Brody took her hand and brought it up to his lips. He kissed her fingertips and then pulled her into a hug.

"Don't start freaking out. We can talk about this. We're worried, too. This is the first for us."

"The first what? Time you shared a woman? That's not what I heard."

"Who told you otherwise?" Ricky asked, sounding angry. Murphy felt that way, too.

"It doesn't matter who. I just need to be sure about this. I want to get to know each of you."

Brody caressed her cheek and she leaned into his palm.

"Baby, last night was incredible."

Murphy could tell that his brothers were feeling on edge. Was she going to break things off before they got started? What was holding her back?

When she wrapped her arms around Brody's waist and held him close, he released a sigh of relief.

"Last night was incredible. I just don't know how a relationship like this can work. The four of you are control freaks."

"Control freaks? Honey, we're leaders. We're set in our ways," Ricky stated.

"I know that and it's going to take some time to get used to. Like today on the phone, Murphy, I told you that we would talk later and you kept pushing. I don't like being pushed." She pulled from Brody's arms.

Brody reached for her hand to stop her.

"Baby, this is new to all of us, too. My brothers and I talked about us last night. We understand what this type of relationship entails. We know what we want and we know we want you. We'll go slow," Brody told her.

Waylon spoke up next, drawing her complete attention to him and his deep voice.

"Don't push us away. Don't run from this."

She was silent and Murphy wondered what was going through her head. "I'll try. I promise."

"How about we work on that dinner while you relax?" Ricky suggested.

She smiled. "I'll just go change and get washed up."

She walked from the room and Murphy looked at his brothers.

"We'll work it out," Brody stated, but Murphy had a bit of an uptight feeling.

* * * *

Amelia freshened up then threw on a light sundress. She hadn't bothered with sandals. As she brushed her hair, she heard her cell phone ringing. At first she felt a twinge of anxiety, hoping that it wasn't Mano. She reached for it, saw the caller ID, and smiled. *Sylvia.*

"Hey you, what's going on?" she asked as she stood in front of the mirror and made sure that she looked okay. Ricky, Brody, Murphy, and Waylon were very attractive men. She felt almost inferior in good looks and great body department. How could any woman resist such attractive men?

"How am I doing? How are you doing, chica? Word is, Mano knows you're in Houston."

"So he knows I'm in Houston. Who cares?"

She turned around and fixed the messy comforter on the bed. She wondered if one of the men had tried to make it this morning, smiling to herself as she thought about the possibility of more mornings like today with them.

"I heard that he called you. I know he did. He was hounding me for your number since the day after you left New York."

"You gave him my number?" Amelia felt her chest tighten. Why would Sylvia do that?

"Hell no! I told that asshole he fucked up with you big-time and that you deserved better. He wasn't too happy, but he did seem determined. He told me about his new gigs and making money legit, ya know?"

"I know."

"He called didn't he? Shit, Amelia, what are you going to do?"

"He can call me all he wants. I won't believe his lies and I won't go down that road again."

"He's determined, Amelia. He hasn't given up on you. He won't give up on you. I'm worried."

"Please don't worry. I'm safe here."

"Well I do worry. So how are the cowboys out there? Any prospects?"

Amelia heard the floor creak and turned to see Waylon standing in the doorway with his arms crossed in front of his chest and a rather upset expression on his face. Did he hear her talking?

"Listen, can I call you later or maybe tomorrow?"

"Oh shit, you have someone there with you now? Damn, girl, you move fast."

"So tomorrow is good, Sylvia?"

"Sure thing. Have fun and live, Amelia. You deserve to live and be free."

"Love you."

"Love you, too."

Amelia disconnected the call then placed the phone on her bedside table. She plugged in the wire.

"Who was that and what did you mean by saying you're safe here?" Waylon asked.

She released a sigh then sat down on the bed. "Listening in on my private conversations?"

"Caring about you is more like it. Who was that?"

She sighed, trying to remember to not make matters worse. She wasn't ready to bare her soul to them. She wanted to give this relationship a try. She loved being with them.

"My friend Sylvia. She worries about me. I was just telling her about how safe I am here. No worries, ya know?"

Waylon walked further into the room.

One look up into his eyes and she had the feeling he'd heard more of the conversation than he let on.

"I thought I heard you mention a guy."

"Waylon, you shouldn't eavesdrop on people's conversations." She stood up, prepared to argue with him if it kept him from making her talk about the phone call. He grabbed her hips and held her in place.

His expression was hard as he stared at her lips. Instantly, she was turned on by him. She had to admit that she loved the feel of his hands on her, and his aggressiveness, which should actually scare the crap out of her. She must be a glutton for punishment.

"Are you hiding something from us?"

It felt like a punch to her gut. He nailed it on the head and her response, though nonverbal, said it all.

"Damn, Amelia, you can trust us. If you're in trouble or if you're running from something."

She shook her head. "Waylon, stop it. Stop trying to force this control on me."

He gave her hips a shake. "Force control on you? Amelia, I care deeply about you. Trust does not come easy for me or my brothers and I get the feeling that it doesn't come easy for you either."

"It doesn't. I'm fine though. There's no need to worry."

She felt his hands caress her hip bones and then move down lower and over her ass. His expression was intense, but she couldn't turn away from him. She licked her lower lip, and he flinched in response.

"Arms up," he ordered, and damn, her body instantly reacted in a positive way.

"Waylon."

"Arms. Up. Now."

She felt her belly quiver as she slowly raised her arms up into the air.

He bent down. She closed her eyes as his hands caressed down the sides of her thighs. In a flash he pulled her dress up and over her head.

She was only wearing panties, and the dress didn't leave room for a bra, even a strapless one.

Her breasts bounced, and immediately he wrapped one strong arm around her waist and lifted her up.

She held on to his arms and shoulders as he placed her down on the bed. Kneeling between her legs, hovering above her, he stroked a finger between her thighs. Back and forth, he trailed that long, thick digit as he stared down into her eyes.

"You're gorgeous. I missed you today, and I want you."

"I missed you, too," she admitted.

He stopped touching her, stood up, and pulled off his shirt, then undid his pants. She stared as each piece of clothing came off of him and more perfect, muscular flesh appeared.

His tattoos were bold and colorful as they trailed down and over his shoulder and upper arm.

The sight of his long, thick cock aroused her senses, and when he reached for her panties, she lifted her hips to aid him.

He tore them off then lowered his shoulders between her thighs.

"Open for me. I want some of your sweet cream, Amelia."

He used the palms of his hands to spread her open, and a moment later his tongue was at her entrance, flicking and sucking her clit.

She grabbed a hold of his head as his relentless strokes brought her closer and closer to orgasm.

"Waylon. Oh God, Waylon, what are you doing?"

He nipped her clit and she gave a small squeal until he pulled from her pussy, grabbed a hold of her hips, and brought her down closer to the edge of the bed. He remained standing over her then aligned his cock with her entrance and shoved inside.

She moaned as she shook from the instant invasion. The feel of his thick long shaft shoving into her wet, hot folds made her release a sigh of pure relief. She wanted him so badly. Having Waylon inside of her actually brought her instant peace and security. *How fucking odd.*

Waylon leaned over her, gripping her hips as she wrapped her legs around his midsection best she could. He was thick, hard, and muscular everywhere as she tried to get closer against him.

He cupped her breasts and tweaked her nipples over and over again, torturing her. Her moans became louder, and she knew the others would hear her. She wanted them here, too. It was so strange to think of the others as Waylon fucked her.

He raised her hips higher, placed his hands on her shoulders, and pushed down as he thrust into her upward. His cock felt as if it hit her womb with every stroke.

She burned inside. Her mind absorbed every bit of desire for this man and for his brothers. It irked her. It excited her and scared the living crap out of her. She wanted to be their possession. She wanted them to own her, brand her, and take her to this feeling of completion at every opportunity they could get. She never felt like this. It was so wild and intense.

"Oh God, Waylon. Harder, harder, Waylon," she demanded.

He pressed his entire body against her. He was crushing her as he used both hands to squeeze her ass cheeks open while thrusting into her cunt. She hugged him to her, hardly capable of breathing a full breath because of his weight and his thrusts. She breathed in his scent. She absorbed the feel of hard, muscular male surrounding her. He was so big, and capable, it made her cunt leak with admiration.

"Fuck, Amelia. I'm coming. Come with me." He growled at her as he stroked her cunt hard. She gripped him tight and counterthrust against him.

"Waylon!" She screamed as her body convulsed underneath him. She felt Waylon tense then explode inside of her.

They panted for air and all she could do was lie there beneath him and relish in the satisfaction of feeling safe with Waylon inside of her.

Would he really keep me safe? Would it really feel like this forever, or one day would he love me less and less?

That painful thought brought her back to reality and immediately that safeguard, that imaginary wall, began to rise back up inside of her.

A moment later he rolled to his side, taking her along with him, causing her to gain full breaths of air. Although he practically crushed her with his weight, she didn't care. She wanted to feel as close as humanly possible to him. She kissed along his collarbone and neck as he caressed her lower back.

"You can really get under my skin," he teased.

"You can really get under mine," she retorted then smiled.

"Um, dessert usually comes after dinner," Ricky teased as he and Brody stood in the doorway smirking.

"I wanted dessert first," Amelia stated boldly. The men raised their eyebrows in surprise.

"Well why didn't you say so in the first place?" Ricky asked as he pulled off his shirt and began to undress. Amelia blushed, but didn't take her eyes off of Ricky. His light blue eyes sparkled, and the more skin, muscles, and tattoos that appeared, the more aroused she became.

Waylon smacked her ass. "Get up on all fours." He slid down off the bed and adjusted her body. He grabbed a light hold of her hair. She turned toward him, stimulated once again, by Waylon's dominant behavior.

Locking gazes with him, she licked her lips then felt Ricky move in behind her. His cock tapped against the crack of her ass and her pussy. She closed her eyes and released a low moan.

"You're going to find yourself in this position, a lot," Ricky said, caressing a palm over her back then over her ass.

Waylon leaned forward and kissed her lips. It was a very sensual, arousing kiss that made her nipples harden and her pussy moisten in preparation for Ricky's cock.

Waylon released her lips as Ricky slowly pushed his cock into her pussy from behind. She heard Ricky moan.

"Home. You feel like home, Amelia." Ricky remained still, deep within her.

Waylon caressed her cheek. "Soon, we're going to take you together."

Ricky pulled out then thrust right back in. Ricky held her hips and continued to stroke her pussy with his cock.

She felt her breath catch in her throat.

Take me together? I don't know if I'll ever be the same after that. I don't know what to do. He feels so good. This feels so right to me.

Her lips parted and Waylon caressed a thumb along them. Then Brody appeared in front of her.

He was naked, too, and holding his cock, bringing it closer to her lips.

"Maybe while Waylon fucks your ass and Ricky fucks your pussy, I'll stick my dick in this pretty little mouth of yours while we fill you and make you ours."

Brody spoke in such a deep, primal tone, Amelia moaned. "Oh God." She lowered her head and felt the eruption inside of her. Her body shook and then Waylon gripped her hair again and tilted her face up toward him.

"Do you want that?"

"I never did anything like that before," she admitted, her voice cracking as she spoke.

"Good," Murphy stated from the doorway. She looked toward him as Waylon released his hold on her.

"'Cause while I watch my brothers make love to you and claim you, I'll go last. Just as you think you can't take any more loving, any more acts of our commitment and possession of you, I'll make love to you, slowly, deeply, Amelia, and secure the bond between us."

She swallowed hard then felt Brody's fingers beneath her chin. She looked toward him and he pressed his cock closer, indicating what he wanted. She wanted it, too. She wanted everything they promised. She wanted to have them around her, all inside of her.

Waylon began to move.

She glanced at him as Ricky pulled out then slowly pushed back into her pussy.

"Stay," she whispered.

Waylon caressed her hair, and then she opened her mouth and stuck her tongue out to take a taste of Brody's cock.

* * * *

Ricky allowed Amelia to adjust to Brody's cock in her mouth. Once she seemed to feel comfortable, he worked on finding his own release and claiming Amelia so she would never want to leave them. His thoughts were obviously just as possessive and wanton as his brothers'. Waylon watched in admiration and stroked Amelia's back. Brody caressed her hair and cheeks as she sucked him, and Murphy stood by the doorway, watching over them. He was the oldest and always acted like they were his responsibility and they each loved him for that.

Ricky continued to pump his hips, and then Amelia moaned, making Brody grunt, and that set Ricky off. He increased his strokes, thrusting deeply until he could no longer stop his body from erupting.

Brody moved faster, Amelia tightened up, and then Brody growled as he climaxed. Ricky followed suit, rubbing her ass cheeks, imagining fucking her ass.

"Amelia!" Ricky yelled then held himself within her.

He could hear her breathing heavy and felt her body shaking. She could hardly keep upright.

"So beautiful. All ours, Amelia. You, every part of you is ours," Brody whispered then leaned down to kiss her.

Ricky pulled slowly from her body as Amelia lowered to the bed.

* * * *

Murphy discarded his clothing then approached the bed. He winked at Ricky who looked extremely happy and then to Brody who was actually smiling. When he locked gazes with Waylon, who caressed Amelia's back as she rested, he saw the seriousness in his brother's eyes. Would Waylon ever smile and let down that wall around his heart? Could Amelia help heal him?

He reached down and caressed her back then lifted her up.

"Oh God, I can't move," Amelia whispered.

Murphy gently lifted her up and into his arms. When she looked at him, she appeared satisfied and tired.

"Remember what I said before?" he asked her, very seriously. He knew he sounded older, but that was his way. He demanded a lot and expected a lot from people. But mostly he wanted respect.

She looked him in the eyes. "You were serious?"

He had to hide his smile. She was perfect. She was amazing.

"Oh, very serious."

He began to walk her into the bathroom.

The feel of her in his arms, the overwhelming need to provide safety, security, and love for her, flooded his system.

He set her down on the counter then reached into the shower to start the water.

When he turned to look at her, she was staring at him. Her eyes roamed over his body.

He towered over her, especially in the small bathroom. He'd have to duck to get under the spray of the water, but his concern was over Amelia, not him. She would come first now. She would take precedence over everything and everyone else.

He walked closer and caressed the palms of his hands up her toned thighs. He looked over her tattoo.

"Why did you pick this? Why one so intricate?"

He traced along the vines and around the flowers with his finger.

She laughed then pushed his hand away.

"Ticklish?" he asked and she nodded her head.

He leaned forward and kissed her. That kiss grew deeper as he pulled her up into his arms. She kissed him back, rubbing her hands along his shoulders and neck, then cupped his cheeks between her palms. He allowed her control of the kiss as he stepped under the spray of the water. He was right. As he predicted, he wouldn't fit under the shower spray so he turned Amelia so that her back faced the wall. He wanted to feel every inch of her. He used his palms to caress over her ass as he lowered her feet to the tub floor.

Barefoot, he saw how short and petite she was in comparison to him, and that caused an instant protectiveness to overcome him. She had released his lips and now her breasts were even with the middle of his chest

Tilting her head back, raising her arms above her head, he watched in admiration, as the water flowed over her large, plump breasts.

He cupped them with his hands and rubbed his thumbs across the hardened little buds.

She opened her mouth, and the water flowed over her tongue and teeth, and he imagined her sucking on him as she had his brother.

Leaning down, he took a breast into his mouth, swirling his tongue over the areola and nipple.

Amelia moaned then thrust her hips forward.

He released her breast and straightened to grab the soap. Lathering it in his hands as Amelia shampooed her own hair, he absorbed the feel of her toned muscles and shapely figure.

"You have an amazing body, Amelia. There's definition everywhere." Murphy began to soap up her body, paying special attention to her breasts. She rinsed her hair, added conditioner, then rinsed it out while he continued to thoroughly cleanse her.

"Let me get you now," she whispered, reaching her palm between their bodies and next to his hand that held the soap.

He smiled down at her. "Okay."

She took the soap from his hand then he leaned over her, placing his palms against the wall above her head.

She soaped him up thoroughly. She started with his neck and shoulders, then moved across his chest and thighs. His cock jerked to attention as she passed it to soap up his thighs. Was she teasing him on purpose? Didn't the little minx know what she was doing to him?

She maneuvered behind him to soap up his back, his ass, and thighs.

"You have a great body, too, Murphy. Nice ass." She squeezed it.

He wrapped an arm around her waist and pulled her back in front of him.

He pressed his palm against her belly then lower to her cunt. Without hesitation, as he held her gaze, he pressed a digit up into her. Instead of gripping his wrist to stop him, she surprised him by leaning back against the tile wall, palms back, breasts pushed forward as she thrust her pussy against his fingers.

"Amelia?" he asked, surprised at how serious and unsteady his voice sounded.

"Yes?" she replied, holding his gaze.

"I can't hold off. You're driving me insane, baby."

"Then don't, Murphy. Fuck me," she said, shocking him.

He pulled his fingers from her, lifted her up, and pressed his cock up into her pussy in one smooth motion.

She gasped, but held on to his shoulders and thrust downward as he thrust upward.

The sight of her parted lips and the sound of her quick breaths caused him to lose control. He wanted to fuck her so good, so hard that she would never stray or ever leave him and his brothers. It was such a carnal thought, but raw and honest.

"More, Murphy. Harder." She begged of him, killing his ability to take it easy.

"Fuck, Amelia, I don't want to hurt you."

"I want it hard. I want you deep. As deep as you can get. Please, Murphy," she begged, and he felt her fingernails push into his skin and her heels dig into his sides.

He grabbed a hold of her hips, pulled back, then shoved hard and deep into her. Over and over again, he pounded his cock into her pussy as she cheered him on, begged him to go harder, faster. He lost complete control as he grunted and thrust. He grabbed every bit of her he could. He reached around her back and as he thrust his cock into her pussy, he pressed a finger into her ass.

"Oh!" she screamed loudly and he lost it.

"Damn, woman!" He pressed her hard against the tiled wall. They were both panting for breath and she was pulling him tighter, closer against his chest. Was she feeling the deep connection, just like he was? "Feel that baby?"

"Yes."

"It's real. This is real."

"I hope so. Oh God, Murphy, I hope so." She hugged his neck and he wondered why she sounded so unsure and so scared. He and his brothers would need to prove it to her. He couldn't help the bit of uncertainty and his own fear lingering in the back of his mind.

This had to work out. He would never be the same man again.

Chapter 11

Waylon was talking on the phone with his agent, Frankie, as he stared at the computer screen. He was looking at the latest round of opponents. One in particular was moving into position. Some young guy from Chicago. But Waylon still had to fight O'Connor.

"I know. So give me a few weeks. I can make that. I'll start doing my heavy training now. I've been doing the light stuff the last few weeks."

"I know I thought it was a bad idea to cancel that last fight with O'Connor in Vegas, but you were right, it made O'Connor's team up the grand prize," Frank stated.

"I don't want you to schedule any other fights right now. I'll let you know when to schedule something else."

"Hey, what's wrong?"

"Nothing is wrong. Actually, everything is right." Waylon traced a piece of notepad with the pen he held in his hand. His mind was on Amelia.

"Hey, you better stay focused. Are you dating someone?" Frank asked and Waylon told him about Amelia.

"Holy shit. You and your brothers?"

"Yep."

"That's what you've always wanted. She must be damn special to get the four of you to actually be nice."

"Fuck you."

Frank chuckled. "Damn, this sounds very serious."

Waylon shook his head despite the fact that Frank couldn't see him.

He gripped the phone tighter.

"I need to get going. Have Jose, Diver, and Quincy call me to set up coming out here."

"You got it. Those guys love coming out to your ranch and working you in that state-of-the-art gym. Fucking funny to have it all set up in a barn."

"No one knows it's even there. I'll talk to you soon," Waylon said, and then disconnected the call.

He heard a knock on the door. "Come in."

Ricky was there. "What's going on?"

Waylon explained about his upcoming fight.

"So you're going to leave Amelia and us for this?"

"I'm training here. I'm not flying out anywhere else."

"Good. How about the fight? How long will you have to leave?"

"Well, it's going to be a good one. A grand prize of a hundred thousand. I'm fighting O'Connor."

"Holy shit. You've been wanting to fight him for the last year."

"Yeah, well, I had to beat a bunch of other people. He's young, got to the top fast, and fights like a street fighter. I'm going to need some special training. The fucking guy has a mean right hook and does take a lot of cheap shots."

Ricky shook his head. "When are you going to tell Amelia about this?"

"Soon. I'm not sure how she's going to take it. She made that comment about not liking fighters."

"Yeah, well, maybe she means just fighting for no reason and not the sport?"

"Maybe. We'll see. How about we go out to the barn and make sure everything is set up? I've got Jose and the guys coming out in a few days."

"Sounds good to me."

Waylon stood up and grabbed his cell phone. He hoped that Amelia understood. When he thought about telling her, he felt as if she would be upset. She meant the world to him. In fact, this fight might wind up being one of his last ones. He was getting older and getting tired of fighting and being angry inside all of the time. He would wait and see once this fight with O'Connor was over.

* * * *

Every night it was the same routine. Amelia would come home from work to find one or all four Haas brothers waiting for her. The lovemaking intensified, and although wary, she wanted to try anal sex with them. She didn't dare suggest it yet. She was trying to get used to their large cocks and strong personalities. Each of them called her regularly at work. They wanted to know every detail of her day, and they shared their days with her as well.

They kind of flipped out a bit about her going out with Regan, Velma, and some other women on Friday night. But Regan told her brothers that they had to share Amelia.

When she walked out of her bedroom, dressed in a thigh-length, snug-fitting black skirt that flared at the bottom and tapped against her thighs, along with a golden yellow camisole, they looked pissed.

The bling on the black cowgirl boots accentuated her calves and thighs.

She pulled her hair to the side and the long, onyx locks fell directly over the cleavage of the golden yellow top she wore, slightly hiding the deep cleavage.

"What the hell are you wearing?" Waylon asked.

She felt her cheeks warm.

"Damn, Mamma, you look hot," Velma stated aloud and Amelia shook her head.

"You guys look incredible, too," Amelia added as she complimented Velma's deep red tank top and jean skirt as well as Regan's fancy, diamond-studded cowgirl boots.

She felt a large, thick arm come around her waist as Brody pulled her back against him. He inhaled against her neck.

"You smell good. Too good to go out with anyone other than one of us."

She tried to pry his hands off of her then gave up. It was useless. The man was strong.

"Stop fussing. You get to smell this perfume all the time."

She felt the palm of his hand move along her belly. Now Murphy, Ricky, and Waylon stood around them.

"Couldn't you wear something less sexy?" Murphy asked.

"No, she can't. She's sexy no matter what she's wearing. Now leave her alone. We need to head out to meet the others." Regan pushed between her brothers.

Brody reluctantly released her, but not before giving her ass a light smack.

"Hey," Amelia reprimanded.

"Hey yourself. We own that ass," Brody stated very seriously, embarrassing Amelia in front of Regan and Velma.

"We'll watch over her," Velma stated then laughed.

"Yeah right," Murphy replied. Amelia waved good-bye to the men, their scowls indicating that they definitely were pissed off, as she got into Regan's convertible.

* * * *

They arrived at the club and Amelia was listening to Velma talk about Jonas.

"So things are going well then?" Regan asked her sister then took a sip of margarita from her glass.

"Yes. I met his brothers, Felix and Canton." Velma took a sip from her drink and avoided eye contact with Regan.

"Wait. His brothers? Do you mean like a ménage thing? They're interested in that?" Regan whispered. Velma looked at Amelia and then to her sister and nodded.

"Holy shit."

"What, Regan? Like you were never interested in that or engaged in a trial run?" Velma raised her eyebrow, daring her sister to deny it.

"Holy shit. You did, Regan? With who?" Amelia asked her.

"Galen has three brothers. I haven't done anything major yet, but I'm exploring the whole thing." She winked then smiled before taking another sip from her drink.

Velma and Amelia laughed.

"Wow. I can't believe this," Amelia stated.

"Well, we can't believe that you're sleeping with our brothers."

"Velma!" Amelia reprimanded then gave her a tap to her thigh.

"Well, well, well, look what we have here."

They turned toward the voice and instantly Amelia cringed at seeing Tucker. *What an asshole.*

He placed his hand on Velma's shoulder, giving it a squeeze.

Velma pushed it away. "Don't touch me, Tucker."

He moved in behind her and two of his buddies joined them. The creeps eyed Amelia and Regan over.

"Don't be like that, Velma. We could be good together. Better than that lowlife asshole, Jonas."

Velma turned toward him, giving him the evil eye.

"Take a walk, Tucker. None of us are interested in seeing you," Regan stated.

Amelia stood up. "Come on let's walk over there."

One guy placed his hand on her waist. "Come dance with me, sweetheart. I've been watching you all night."

"Get your hands off of her. She's taken," Regan raised her voice.

"Oh yeah, that's right. You're fucking four guys. Why don't you come home with me, Amelia, I'll show you what you're missing. I'm better than all four of those muscle heads," Tucker said.

"You know what, Tucker? You're so typical," Amelia told him.

"Typical of what?"

"Typical of a man who has such a small penis. He needs to overcompensate with his mouth because he can't succeed by performance."

Regan and Velma laughed. So did Tucker's two buddies.

"Come on," Regan said, taking Velma's hand. The three of them walked away, and as Amelia turned around, she could see how angry Tucker was.

As the night continued, Velma and Regan were enjoying themselves, but Amelia kept her eyes on Tucker and his friends. She didn't trust them. She especially didn't like the way Tucker was watching Velma. Although Amelia had warned both Regan and Velma about Tucker's comment to her at work, she was still concerned. After all, someone had already tried forcing themselves on Velma the night of her birthday. Luckily, Jonas was there to help her.

As Amelia excused herself to use the ladies' room, she realized that she actually missed the men. The last week had been incredible. They catered to her, made love to her as soon as she arrived home from work, and they shared dinner together. The best part of all was how the men were easing up telling her about their lives. She understood that they had hard times. She knew firsthand about that. The fact that they shared how Waylon and Brody were adopted and of course how they gained their nicknames, pulled on her heart.

Sam, Jordan, Tysen, and Elise were amazing and their love for their children was commendable. Amelia was envious. Her family life had been filled with nothing but heartache. Considering there were three men in her life after her mom died, all of them had failed her. She had been the one to take care of them. She had been on the receiving end of their anger and their destructive behavior, and she was the one to bury them.

Getting involved with Mano was a huge mistake and she should have followed her gut. Even now, knowing how wonderful Ricky,

Waylon, Brody, and Murphy were, she still feared their wrath, their commanding ways, and ultimately, she feared getting hit by them.

She swallowed hard as she looked in the mirror and felt the need to call them. She pulled out her cell phone and saw the text message from Mano.

It's not over. I'll give you some time to think about us. But you will be mine again, Amelia. I'm not giving you up.

She was instantly angry. Angry at the fact that the man didn't get it. Where had he been the last year? If he had cared, if he had truly made a regrettable mistake by treating her the way he did, and by cheating on her, then where was he? Now, he suddenly wanted her back? She was done with him. She was finished allowing men to control her and use their masculinity.

Amelia took a deep breath then looked up Murphy's cell number, then sent a group message to the four of them. She chuckled as she typed her message. *In order to talk to my boyfriends at once, I need to send a group message.* God, being in a ménage relationship was funny and different. She instantly smiled, as she typed the words "I miss you guys. See you tomorrow."

* * * *

Velma and Regan were waiting in the hallway for Amelia to exit the bathroom. Somehow, Tucker and his buddies cornered them.

"Let go of me, Tucker. I'm not interested in you. Never have been and never will be," Velma said as she tried to pull away from Tucker.

"Release my sister!" Regan yelled as one of Tucker's friends wrapped an arm around her waist and pulled her back against him.

"You got a really sweet body, honey. How about we all go party at our place?" He licked across Regan's neck. Velma watched in horror as Regan tried to pull away.

"Leave her alone," Velma said, pulling from Tucker's hold. He went to grab her and she ducked, but then turned around and caught his fist. She screamed and grabbed her mouth.

"Get away from them."

Velma saw Amelia. She shoved the guy that was holding Regan away as two guys in black followed her. Velma figured they were bouncers as they each grabbed Tucker's two friends.

Amelia approached and Tucker grabbed her hand.

"I'll take you instead." He pulled Amelia to the back exit door. Velma and Regan screamed for help as they tried to stop Tucker.

* * * *

Amelia attempted to pull her hand from Tucker's but it was no use.

"Let go of me. I swear, you'll regret this."

He stopped, pulled her against his chest and gripped her chin.

"I already regret not taking you sooner. You're fucking four guys. You probably like it rough. I got some friends at the house. We'll keep you busy."

He grabbed her hair and pulled her toward his truck. She could hear Velma and Regan screaming in the distance. Something came over her. Fear, anger at being treated this way by another man. One she didn't know and even told him to leave her alone.

"I'm not going with you," she told him and he shoved her hard against the car door. Her hip hit the metal and she felt the sting of pain. Something sharp was on the door. She slapped at his chest and he shoved her back against the car again. She lost her breath, saw the anger in his eyes, and knew she was in serious trouble. *Not again. Never again.*

Tucker pulled open his door and grabbed her. She threw a right hook, hitting his chin. He lowered his shoulder, picked her up, ripping her skirt in the process, and tossed her up and into the truck.

She kicked at him then slid down off the seat and onto the ground, scraping her thigh in the process. She heard screaming and then male voices, when suddenly Regan and Velma attacked Tucker. They were hitting him and pulling him away from Amelia until another two bouncers took over.

"Amelia, are you okay?" Regan asked as she and Velma helped her to stand up.

"Miss, are you okay? An ambulance is on the way," some guy said, and Amelia hugged Regan and Velma.

"Why do these things keep happening to me? Why?" Amelia closed her eyes as the pain began to set in.

* * * *

Amelia refused to go to the hospital to get checked over. She had a large bruise on her lower back after Tucker shoved her against the truck. Her lip was sore and slightly swollen and she had a large scrape from sliding down onto the ground.

The police came and so did the cavalry. By the time she finished signing papers with the police officers along with Regan and Velma to press charges, the men had arrived. Included in the bunch were Jonas and his two brothers as well as Galen and his three brothers.

"Amelia!" Amelia saw Ricky, Murphy, Brody, and Waylon coming toward them. She lowered her eyes and turned toward Regan. Regan placed an arm over her shoulder and Amelia pulled the blanket that the paramedic gave her tighter against her body. When the men saw her injuries, her torn skirt and cuts, they were going to flip out.

"It will be okay," Regan whispered.

"I know. I just want to go home, Regan. My head is pounding," Amelia said.

"Amelia, are you okay?" Murphy asked as he turned her around.

The instant he saw her bloody lip he scowled, his grip a little tighter on her arms.

"Please, Murphy, I'm okay. I swear."

"Who did this?" Waylon raised his voice then looked around, as if the culprit would be standing there.

"Tucker," Regan said as Ricky pulled her into his arms and caressed her hair. Brody was holding Velma.

"Amelia fought him off. He was trying to make Velma leave with him. His two friends were trying to get me to go, too. Amelia came out of the bathroom and stopped them. Then Tucker forced her from the building." Regan was telling the story.

"Forget it. It's over. He's in police custody. Let's leave. Please. I want to go," Amelia said, turning out of Murphy's hold.

They were talking behind her. She heard them, but she didn't care. She just wanted to go home, shower, and get under the covers in bed. She could cover her head and drown out the sounds, the images, and the memories from her past. This reminded her of Mano. His "my way, and nothing else" attitude. When she disobeyed, he was forceful. He always hit something or her.

She swallowed hard and jerked to the side when she felt hands on her waist.

"Baby, it's me. It's only me," Murphy stated.

They got up into the truck. A glance out the window and she saw that Velma was being cared for by Jonas, and who Amelia assumed were his brothers. She was safe now. To the side she saw Waylon talking to Regan, and Regan was speaking a mile a minute as tears rolled down her cheeks. She was surrounded by four men, including Galen. Amelia figured that those were Galen's brothers. Waylon then pointed at Jonas as if demanding he take care of Regan or something, and Jonas nodded his head as he kept an arm around her shoulder.

The flashing lights and the disgusted faces all brought on a surge of emotions and memories she had forced behind her.

Her home life had been no better than her love life at the time. Her brothers and her father were abusive in their own ways. She tightened her eyes, and when the door opened again, Ricky was climbing up in beside her.

"Goddamn it, baby, this could have been a lot worse." He pulled her closer. She cringed from the cut on her thigh and the injury on her lower back. It would surely be bruised by morning or even sooner.

She snuggled into Ricky's arms, remaining still and quiet as Murphy drove her home.

* * * *

Waylon and Brody drove in the SUV. He was so angry he felt his hands shaking. He wanted to hit something, someone, specifically Tucker, for what he had done.

"That slimy bastard. I swear if I see that motherfucker anywhere around Amelia, Regan, and Velma, I'm going to rip his head off."

"Waylon, you need to calm down. Believe me, man, I feel the same fucking way right now. I can't believe he attacked her. Do you think what the cops said was true? Do you think Tucker was high on something?"

Waylon looked at Brody and released a deep sigh.

"I don't give a fuck. I'm just glad I scheduled to train here, or I wouldn't even be here right now and instead too far away to see Amelia."

A beeping sound came from the purse he held on his lap.

"What's that?" Brody asked.

Waylon reached into her purse and saw that her cell phone was vibrating.

Glancing down he saw the phone light up and Regan's name appear.

"It's Regan texting Amelia."

He looked at the message.

What did you mean by these types of things are always happening to you?????

"What does it say?" Brody asked and Waylon told him.

"I don't like the sound of that," Brody added.

Waylon felt entirely too on edge to be kept up in the cab of a vehicle right now. He wanted to hit his punching bag to let off some steam or something. He felt the anger and all his emotions getting the better of him. This was his problem. This was his burden, his weight upon his shoulders day in and day out.

He scanned her other texts and saw the four returned texts from him to his brothers.

"She group messaged us, saying that she missed us tonight. We shouldn't have let her go out. She needs us."

"I know, Brody. I fucking feel the same way. She's a beautiful woman. People take notice of her immediately, and that pisses me off to think that other men are hitting on her. If she's with one of us, that won't fucking happen," Brody stated firmly.

"What do you think the message from Regan means?"

"I don't know. We should ask her."

Waylon scanned up toward earlier texts and as he read the last one before Amelia texted him and his brothers, he felt ready to explode.

"What the fuck?" He raised his voice. Brody immediately asked him what was wrong.

"Some fucking guy texted her."

"What? Who?"

"It's not labeled. The area code is not from around here. I think it's New York."

"What the fuck does it say?"

"She lied to us. She's involved with someone or at least was recently. He wants her back." Waylon slammed his fist down on the dashboard.

"What does it say, Waylon? Tell me now. If she's playing us. My God, Waylon, if she is, I don't know what I'll do. I—"

"The text from the guy says, 'It's not over. I'll give you some time to think about us. But you will be mine again, Amelia. I'm not giving up.'"

Waylon felt the pain in the pit of his stomach, but worse was the one in his heart. The pain in a place he thought was dead.

"Maybe it's not what it seems," Brody said but sounded as if he were trying to convince himself of his own statement.

"Maybe she's just like most women. I'm getting to the bottom of this, immediately."

* * * *

Amelia got out of the truck as Murphy opened the front door. Ricky helped her to go inside.

"I'm going to go take shower."

She walked directly to her bedroom.

"Amelia!" She heard Waylon's voice and swiftly turned toward the bedroom door. He looked enraged. His eyes were dark and angry, his fists by his side, and Brody stood beside him, arms crossed and appearing just as pissed off. The tears hit her eyes as her belly quivered in fear. They blamed her for this.

"Who the fuck is the guy?" Waylon yelled as he stomped toward her. Amelia was shocked at the anger in his voice as her back pressed against the wall behind her. The blanket dropped from her body. She saw Murphy and Ricky looking concerned and Brody was in a dead stare at her ripped skirt.

"Don't hit me. Please don't hit me." She cried and slowly lowered to the floor.

"Who is he?" Waylon yelled from a few feet away.

"Waylon, you're scaring her," Ricky stated as he moved toward her.

"Get away. Get away from me, all four of you. Just go. Leave me now. I don't want to see you."

"Who is he?" Brody asked this time.

"What are you two talking about?" Ricky asked.

"What the hell is going on with you two?" Murphy asked.

Waylon passed over her cell phone and Amelia realized that they'd seen the message from Mano.

"This fucking guy texted her," Brody stated.

She didn't even hear their exchange of words between one another. All she could focus on was Waylon's and Brody's anger and the way Waylon looked as if he were going to strike her. Was he capable of that, or was she so scared because of her past, that she couldn't give him, them, the chance.

"I'm not going down this road again. I won't be a punching bag. Get out. I don't want to ever see you again. Get out!"

"A punching bag? This guy struck you?" Waylon asked.

"Explain it to us, Amelia. Help us understand," Murphy whispered as he knelt down on the rug.

She looked at him through blurry vision. She shook her head. "It doesn't matter. Pain is all I'll ever feel."

Murphy reached for her and she felt so exhausted from crying, from the episode with Tucker, and now a confrontation with Waylon and Brody. She closed her eyes and he lifted her up and carried her to the bed.

Murphy caressed the tears from her eyes, and Ricky placed a blanket over her body. They more than likely didn't want to see the torn skirt.

She shifted to her side and cringed.

"You're hurt," Ricky said then knelt on the bed and reached for her camisole. He raised it up and cursed at the sight.

"We need ice. Go get ice, Brody."

She caught sight of Waylon standing behind Murphy. He looked irate.

"Look at me, Amelia," Murphy whispered as he caressed her cheek. She wanted to be held by him, by *them*, so badly, she felt the tear roll down her cheek. But how could she? They obviously had anger issues, and Waylon and Brody looked capable of crossing the line. If one of them hit her, she wouldn't be able to take it.

"We're all upset about what happened tonight. Perhaps if you explain the texts, Brody and Waylon can understand."

"They want to hit me, Murphy. If you and Ricky weren't here, then Waylon and Brody would have hit me."

"That's not true. I would never hit you," Waylon stated firmly. "Fuck, Amelia, I'm so pissed off right now. Tell me who the guy is. Tell us what the hell is going on."

She stared at him. She wanted to believe that he would have never struck her, but she was having difficulty believing him. "I have the ice," Brody said. As Ricky reached for the bag of ice, Brody shook his head. "Let me."

Ricky moved from the bed and Brody leaned closer to her. She looked at him, and when he reached for her, her breath hitched.

He touched her cheek. He caressed it softly with his fingers.

"I swear, baby. I swear that my brothers and I would never hit you or hurt you in any way. We care about you so much, Amelia. The thought that some guy tried to take you and that he hit you and hurt you enraged us. We saw a text message from Regan asking why you said these things keep happening to you."

"Then we read the one from the guy," Waylon said next. "The one texting that he was giving you time and that things weren't over between you two. We both lost it. We both feared that you were cheating on us. Please tell us what's going on. We'll work it out."

This was a moment of great risk for Amelia. She stared at the four men she had grown to love in such a short period of time. Her past was ruining her future, and either these men were for real and honestly wouldn't hurt her or she was destined for a future of pain and heartache. It seemed to her that the greatest fight she ever had was within herself. Could she believe them? Could she trust that what they were saying that they felt was true?

She shook with reservations and fear. She felt so hollow and lonely inside. She had been used to that sensation until these men came along. They filled that empty gap inside of her. They completed her. But she feared that could all be a lie.

This was the fine line between believing in these men and the gut instinct telling her that they were sincere, or letting her fear, her distrust, destroy a future with them.

"I need the ice on my back. I don't want it to swell," she whispered, Brody softly placed the bag of ice on her lower back where the bruise was.

She closed her eyes and took a deep breath.

When she opened her eyes, they were all watching her.

"His name is Mano. I am not cheating on you. I left him over a year ago, and until recently, he hadn't pursued me. Before I left New York, I visited my friend Sylvia and her grandmother. His brother, Escala, saw me and called Mano. He tried to convince me to hang out, and of course I refused. He somehow got my cell phone number, and so he keeps texting and he called once. That's it."

"Murphy." Waylon said his brother's name and Murphy moved out of the way and off the bed. Waylon sat down next to her. He reached for her chin and gently brushed his thumb across her skin, below the cut on her lip. "I swear, I would never hit you. I was angry, yes, and all my life I've used my fists to express my emotions. But, I would never hit you, Amelia. I promise you. Trust me please."

"Do you trust me, Waylon? Do you believe that I'm not involved with Mano?"

"If you say that it is over and that this guy is bothering you, then I believe you."

"I wouldn't survive it if you or your brothers ever hurt me like he did. I wouldn't," she said as a tear rolled down her cheek.

"Never, Amelia. Never." He leaned forward, and kissed her cheeks, avoiding her lips.

He lay down beside her and placed a hand over her belly as she held his gaze. Brody lifted the ice away and kissed her shoulder.

"Amelia, who was the guy in the picture in that blue bin?" Murphy asked as he and Ricky sat down on the bottom of the bed.

She felt her stomach tighten. She needed to explain everything to them. If they hated her, or thought the worse, then so be it.

"There's so much to explain."

"Take your time. We're not going anywhere, Amelia. We're here for you, forever," Ricky said as he caressed her calf. She could feel the warmth of his skin penetrate through the blanket. Her love for him and his brothers couldn't be smothered or minimized in any way. She had to tell them about her past. She needed to start trusting people again, so why not her lovers?

* * * *

Waylon felt so damn shitty inside right now. He scared Amelia to the point in which she actually thought he would hit her. *What the fuck? Who hurt my woman? Who put fear in her like this?*

"Start at the beginning," Murphy whispered.

All of them were touching her and caressing her over the blanket. Waylon was staring right down into her eyes. She was the most beautiful, sexy woman he had ever laid eyes on. The moment he saw her, despite his own fears, he wanted to get to know her better. The fact that he was showing such emotion was completely unlike him. He could also see the changes in his brothers. Murphy, the oldest and most demanding, was softer and calmer around Amelia. Ricky had eased up to her quickly. It was like he was the least resistant to opening up his heart to her. Waylon had never seen his brothers act this way. And Brody, Brody shocked the shit out of him. He hated having scars. He was self-conscious about it. He and Ricky felt comfortable enough to be around Amelia with nothing on, and she didn't stare at their scars or ask questions or pry.

When Amelia saw Brody, her reaction was sincere. She didn't look at him in disgust, but instead with compassion. She told him she understood what it felt like and that she had scars of her own. Now they would understand what she meant.

"I guess I'll start with telling you guys why I was so resistant accepting your advances."

"Our advances, huh?" Ricky teased.

She smiled as she lowered her eyes. "The four of you represent everything that I'm afraid of and everything that I'm familiar with. You see, my father and two brothers, Kyle and Edward, were in the military. Edward died in combat. He was captured and killed. When Kyle was discharged, he had problems."

"What kind of problems?" Brody asked.

"Psychological problems. PTSS, paranoia, and violent behavior."

"Was he abusive to you, Amelia?" Murphy asked, looking very upset at the possibility. Waylon felt his own chest tighten and rage filled his heart.

She nodded her head. "I tried hard to help them."

"Them?" Ricky asked.

Amelia lowered her eyes then sat up against the headboard. The blanket fell and the strap of her camisole fell from her shoulder, and she pulled it back into place.

"I had been taking care of my father. My mom died a few years before Kyle's return and months after Edward was killed. She couldn't handle it. Plus, my dad was in the military, too. He was a real hard-ass and didn't accept failure. He was abusive, and he turned to alcohol to ease the pain."

"Jesus!" Murphy stated.

"What happened to Kyle?"

"He chose the wrong path, Waylon. He thought that fighting and doing drugs eased the pain. He was a fighter, like you. He boxed a lot, but illegally mostly."

Waylon felt sick to his stomach. It very well could have been him. Aside from never turning to drugs or painkillers and alcohol to ease his bad memories, he did take his anger out in the ring. No wonder she was so scared.

"I'm not like that. I've never done drugs and I don't drink a lot, just casually," Waylon told her.

"I didn't say that you did, Waylon. Mano is a boxer, too."

"What?" Brody asked, turning Amelia by her chin up toward him so he could look her in the face.

"Kyle and Mano were friends. Mano served in the military, too. He and his brother were discharged and stripped of their ranks."

"We were all in the military, Amelia. All of us were Special Forces. Don't think for a moment that we would disrespect our profession, our commitment to the Corps, or this country," Brody stated firmly.

She reached up and ran the palm of her hand up his chest. "I would never do that. I know the difference. In every profession there are good and bad people. I just saw the worse of them. I should have learned to stay away from such aggressive men. Mano was controlling. My brother was fighting for him and with him in the ring. The night Kyle died, he was high. He was getting killed in the illegal fight and Mano didn't stop it. There was a lot of money riding on it. I found out later that Mano bet against Kyle. He probably even supplied him with the drugs that ultimately made his heart explode."

"What an asshole. How did you get away from him? What did you do?" Murphy asked.

"I was so angry. But I was also scared of Mano's temper."

"You said he hit you? How often?" Waylon asked. He was biting the inside of his cheek. He wanted to take all those bad memories away from her. He wanted to erase them from his mind and he felt like such an asshole for getting so angry with her earlier. No wonder she was scared.

"Months. But when I found out about Kyle, the drugs, and that Mano bet against him, I went to confront him. He was the only family I had left and now there was no one to trust. No man to lean on for support to protect me and care for me. I wanted someone to love me and I wanted it all to be a misunderstanding."

He watched as Amelia took a deep breath and wiped the tear from her eye before it fell.

"What happened?" Ricky asked.

"I went to the apartment to talk with him. I made the decision that if he truly did those things and caused Kyle's death, then we were finished. When I got there—"

She stopped talking and swallowed hard as she closed her eyes and shook her head.

"Yes?" Brody asked.

"I found him in bed with two women."

"Holy shit," Murphy said. She nodded her head.

"What did he do? What did he say?" Brody asked.

"He blamed it all on me. He told me that I was crazy and then he beat me."

"Holy fuck."

Waylon pulled her into his arms and against his chest. He kissed the top of her head and caressed her upper back, being sure to watch out for her injuries. His heart ached for her. Twenty-six years old and she had more than a lifetime's worth of agony and heartache.

"I'm so sorry, Amelia. I'm sorry that you were all alone and that you went through all of that. Mostly, I'm sorry that I made you feel like he made you feel."

She tilted her head toward him and cupped his face between her hands. He could see the tears glistening on her thick, long eyelashes. "No, Waylon. We both behaved wrongly. It was my insecurities and fears from being hurt by Mano that have made me resistant to trusting all of you, and giving this relationship a chance. You started yelling, and charging at me, believing the worse, before fully understanding the situation. I know in my heart that you, Murphy, Brody, and Ricky would never hurt me. The only way you could do that was if you pushed me away and told me that you didn't want me anymore because of all of this."

"Are you kidding me? We want to take all the pain away," Ricky stated.

"We want to help you to forget about all of it," Murphy told her.

"We want to love you and we want you to love us and trust us," Brody said as he leaned over her shoulder then kissed her skin.

"I'm already in love with you, Amelia. Tonight proves it. My heart's been cold and broken for far too long. But when I found out that you were in trouble, I lost it. Then add in the misunderstanding about the text message and forget it. I was a wild man with jealousy, anger, and devastation. I don't want to ever feel that way again. You complete me, Amelia."

"I love you, too, Waylon." She wrapped her arms around his neck and kissed him. He kissed her back, rolled her to her back, and gave her everything he had. When he released her lips, she cringed, and he saw the cut on her lip.

"I'm sorry."

"No. I needed that kiss. My lips will heal. I promise to be honest with you all from now on."

"Us, too," Ricky stated.

"Now, what are we going to do about that Mano character?" Murphy asked. Waylon had forgotten about him for a moment.

"Kill the fucker," Brody stated very seriously and they all laughed.

Amelia turned to her left to look at Brody. "Thanks for that."

Brody smiled then ran the palm of his hand up her belly, under the camisole to her breast. He cupped the mound and she parted her lips. "You're our woman. We'll protect you." He leaned down to kiss her lips.

Waylon felt the concern remain inside of him. Something told him that this situation was far from over. A bit more information and some phone calls to their friends might be needed.

"We'll need some information on him. We've got friends that can help," Waylon whispered.

"Could we talk about it later? My head is throbbing and I feel very tired," Amelia said.

"Sure thing, sweetheart. You can sleep in tomorrow," Waylon told her.

"I probably won't have a job by Monday morning," Amelia stated.

"Why not?" Murphy asked.

"Because Tucker is my boss's son."

"Toby knows his son is a jerk. When the cops prove that he was high or whatever and the charges stick, Toby will do the right thing," Ricky said with confidence.

"I sure hope so, or I'm going to have to look for a job and move back in with Regan. That will totally cramp the girl's love life."

"Could we not talk about our sister's love life please?" Murphy replied.

"The only other place you would move in would be our place. We'll work it out. You get some rest," Brody told her and she smiled then snuggled closer into the pillow. She held Brody's hand against her breast and then leaned into Waylon. Waylon looked at Murphy and Ricky and smiled then winked.

They would work it all out. Protecting Amelia was their top priority now, and no one was going to try and tear them apart. No one.

Chapter 12

Amelia awoke with a start. She absorbed the smell of men's cologne and the feel of warmth cocooning her. She tried to adjust her eyes to the dim light of the room as she lifted her head and cringed just a little.

Brody was holding her from behind. His large hand covered her breast. Waylon was right next to her on her other side. His expression seemed angry, even in sleep. She searched for Murphy and Ricky, and didn't find them. Perhaps they went to go sleep on the couch. It was early morning. A glance by the table and her clock read 4:45 a.m.

Suddenly the hand that cupped her breast moved, and Brody gave it a squeeze. She smiled to herself as she turned slightly to look at him over her shoulder, but couldn't see if he had his eyes open.

She loved them all so much. Last night was scary, but ended with good stuff. Sharing her fears with them was necessary. Now it was time to move on. She would deal with the Tucker incident on Monday.

She placed her hand over Brody's and moved it lower. At first, he resisted, probably thinking that she wanted it away from her breast. *No way. I would never push away their touch, their masculinity, and show of affection. I crave it now. I want to feel them everywhere, especially inside of me.*

She pushed it over her belly then down between her legs. He cupped her pussy over the material of the skirt. As she started to roll to her back, to give him better access to her body, he moved his hand down and under the material.

His fingers maneuvered under her panties. She moved her hand down over his and spread her thighs wider. As she followed the motions his fingers took, she moaned. She was touching herself, with Brody. It was erotic and made her want him inside of her.

Another hand moved along her camisole. *Waylon.*

He kissed her shoulder, leaned up on his elbow, then looked down to where his brother stroked her pussy.

"You want us?"

"Always," she replied, and he held her expression with such intensity she nearly released a small cry of pleasure.

"Let us take you together," Brody whispered, adjusting his body and pressing his fingers in and out of her pussy faster. She gripped his wrist and released a small spasm of pleasure as she thrust her breasts upward.

"Yes."

Brody gently pulled fingers from her pussy then began to help Waylon discard her clothing from her body. She tensed a few times as they adjusted her to their liking.

"Are you in pain?" Waylon asked as he wrapped an arm around her from behind and lifted her up.

"No. With you, only pleasure."

He kissed along her collarbone then her shoulder.

"We'll go slow. We don't have any lube on us. I'll need to get this sexy ass of yours ready. You just relax and enjoy this. Taking you like this binds our commitment to you and you to us even further. Do you understand?" Waylon, so very serious and intense, made her shake with both anticipation and reservations.

Would it be pleasurable, or was the hype better than the actual act? She was so aroused and so wet right now it didn't matter. She wanted them everywhere.

"I want it. I want you both. I want to feel safe and loved. I'm tired of being scared, Waylon. I'm tired of feeling incomplete."

"Come to me, baby," Brody said. Waylon lifted her up and placed her on a now fully naked Brody. She licked her lips, feeling the sting from the cut there. Brody caressed her cheek then ran a thumb gently below the wound.

"Does it hurt a lot?" he asked as he adjusted his hips.

She shook her head.

Waylon pressed a finger to her pussy. It slid right in because she was so damn wet.

"Jesus, baby, you're soaked," he told her. She closed her eyes and moaned as the tiny little spasms of pleasure released. She sure was wet, as he moved his finger from pussy to anus, coating the puckered hole with her own cream.

"Oh God, Waylon, I feel so aroused."

"I love it baby. I love you, and how you get all wet and ready for our cocks. This ass is mine, darling," he whispered, pressing against her. Keeping one hand on her shoulder, he squeezed as he pressed his finger through the tight rings of her ass. Back and forth he rotated the digit, and she moaned then reached for her cunt.

Brody gently moved her fingers from her own clit. "Allow me, darling." She locked gazes with him as Brody stroked her cunt while Waylon thrust his finger back and forth into her anus.

She began to press back then ride their fingers.

"I need you," Brody whispered, then pulled her to him and kissed her lips. Waylon released his hold on her shoulder, as Brody pulled his fingers from her cunt.

He then moved his hands over her hips and lifted her so that she could take his cock inside of her.

She lifted up, felt the small bit of ache in her lower back, then eased down his shaft.

Brody held her gaze.

"Just like that. Inside of you is heaven, Amelia. Pure heaven."

She moaned, tilting her head back, moving her pelvis, trying to get him deeper inside of her. She began to ride him, thrusting up and down as quickly as she could,

Brody grabbed her hips. "Slow down, baby, or I'll come before Waylon is inside of you."

At that moment she felt Waylon's hands on her back and his fingers trailing back and forth over the crack of her ass, while his other finger moved smoothly in and out of her ass.

"You're sopping wet, Amelia. It's dripping from your pussy." Waylon pressed a finger against her puckered hole. She moaned then thrust harder onto Brody's cock.

"That's it, baby. You like this don't you? You want to try this? You want both of us together?"

"Yes, oh God, Waylon, please." She felt another eruption. The sloshing sound filled the room.

Waylon pressed her back down so she was chest to chest with Brody. Brody grabbed her face between his hands and kissed her. She could feel Waylon's fingers press through the tight rings of her ass. It burned as she moaned into Brody's mouth and tensed from the odd invasion.

"Keep moving. Just relax your muscles. You're so tight, baby. You're sucking my fingers in deeper. Your body knows. You want it." He began to move his fingers in and out of her ass again, and she knew he was getting her ready for his cock. He was a big man they all were in that department. She tensed a moment until Brody thrust upward.

Amelia felt this deep pull inside of her pussy and core. It was like some sort of imaginary string. With every stroke of Waylon's fingers, she opened her thighs wider and began to move on Waylon. Brody caressed her ass cheek with his free hand.

"That's it, baby. Ride him."

"Oh God, Waylon, do something. I need more." She raised her voice and Waylon pulled his fingers from her ass. Her body erupted and she moaned then thrust up and down on Brody's cock.

"Here I come," Waylon said. She felt the tip of his cock at her back opening. She tensed a moment. Fear gripped her insides. He was a big man. Fingers were one thing, but Waylon's thick, hard cock was another.

Brody grabbed her face between the palms of his hands.

"Look at me. Look at me and feel the love between us. We'd never hurt you. This is all we've ever dreamed about."

She lowered slightly, adjusted her pussy, and felt Waylon push into her anus.

"Oh God, Waylon. Oh my God." She raised her voice and he pushed all the way inside of her. She gasped for air. Brody cupped her breasts and pulled so hard on her nipples that she gasped and momentarily forgot about the burning sensation behind her.

"I'm in. Holy fuck, you're so damn tight. I'm going to come quick, Amelia," Waylon told her. Then they began to move. She moaned and initially felt tense but with every thrust from them back and forth, she became so aroused and so needy she begged for more.

"How does it feel?" Brody asked.

"More. I want more. Please do something."

They were touching her, caressing her, pulling on her nipples, and gripping her ass and hips. They were surrounding her as Brody exploded and she followed after. "Oh!" She moaned loudly and then Waylon pulled out and shoved back into her ass. She lost her breath on each of his strokes, then felt his fingers dig into her hips as he thrust one final time, held her hips in place, and moaned against her shoulder.

They were all panting for air.

"That was fucking sexy as damn hell to watch," Ricky stated as Amelia looked over her shoulder to see Ricky and Murphy standing in the doorway wearing their boxers.

Slowly Waylon pulled from her ass, making her gasp. "I'll get something to clean you up." He kissed her shoulder.

Brody pulled from her next then rolled her to her back. He kissed her softly on the lips then lower, trailing kisses over her very sensitive breasts and nipples.

The light from outside was beginning to fill the room. It was still early, but the sun was rising.

"You look like a goddess," Murphy stated then walked closer to the bed.

Waylon returned and began to wash her.

"I can do that," she said and reached for the cloth.

He gave her a stern expression. "I'll take care of you."

"It's our job now," Brody whispered then nipped her nipple.

"Hey," she scolded him, swatting him away. But Waylon moved and Murphy lifted her up toward him. He had removed his boxers and now sat on the edge of the bed with her straddling his hips. They moved her around like a rag doll and she loved it. It gave her such a feminine feeling. They would take care of her.

* * * *

Murphy was overwhelmed with emotions. He ran his fingers through her hair then kissed her on the mouth. He felt Amelia reach for his cock. When her delicate fingers wrapped around his shaft, he moaned.

She lifted her hips and aligned his cock with her pussy. She felt wet and ready as she slowly lowered herself onto him.

"You're so beautiful and sexy. You scared me last night."

Her head was slightly tilted back as she lowered up and down on him. Her lips were parted, and her breasts were full and plump. He moved his hands along her lower back and everywhere he could reach.

"Damn, baby, you got my dick so hard right now."

She tensed a moment when Ricky touched her from behind.

"Are you okay?" Murphy asked.

"No," she whispered and he immediately felt tense. He scrunched his eyes and Ricky placed his hands on her shoulder.

"What's wrong?" Ricky asked her.

She tilted her head up toward Ricky and leaned her back against him. Her breasts were fully accessible and her expression serious as she looked up, holding Ricky's gaze.

"I need you inside me, too, Ricky. I want to bind us all together, like I did with Waylon and Brody."

Murphy saw Ricky smile then smooth his hands down over Amelia's breasts, cupping them and fondling them.

He thrust his hips against her ass and Amelia released a bit of cream.

"With pleasure, Amelia," Ricky said then massaged her breast again before moving his hands slowly up her body, over her shoulders then to her back.

Amelia leaned forward and pushed Murphy to his back. His legs spread over the edge of the bed and Murphy knew she wanted it.

She gripped Murphy's shoulders and began to move atop of him. Up and down she stroked his cock and Murphy closed his eyes and relished in the sensation of being inside of her.

He gripped her hips, needing deeper penetration. She was going too slow.

"Damn, woman, you feel so good." He thrust upward and she gasped from the move. He did it again, and he felt the cream release from her pussy. She was so turned on and wet from this. She was feeling what he was. He just knew it.

The sloshing sound filled the room and then Ricky pressed her chest lower.

"Damn baby, you look so sexy. Your cream is glistening between your thighs. Your ass is so perfect," he told her then swiped his finger over the cream and pressed it to her anus. He repeated the motion and then leaned down and licked between her ass cheeks.

"Oh, Ricky. Oh." She moaned then thrust down and back, spreading herself wider for them.

"Nice and easy. Just like Waylon," Ricky said, and Amelia kissed Murphy. She explored his mouth and Murphy enjoyed the way she made love to him. He knew the moment that Ricky breached her ass. Amelia tightened, then pressed her tongue deeper, kissed him harder, as she thrust back against Ricky.

Ricky moaned then gripped her hips.

"Slow down. I'll come before I can even enjoy this tight ass." He gave her a smack on her cheek and Amelia pulled her mouth from Murphy's.

Murphy felt her cream again.

"Damn, I think our woman likes to get spanked."

"Oh God." Amelia moaned as she tried to counter their thrusts.

Murphy heard Ricky smack her ass again.

"You like that? You like being a naughty girl and getting this ass of yours fucked and smacked at the same time?"

"Oh God, Ricky, I can't take it. Never. I never thought it could be like this." She moaned and thrust her pussy down hard over Murphy's cock, then pulled up and thrust back against Ricky's cock.

"Holy shit, Amelia," Murphy said then exploded inside of her as he gripped her hips, making her remain still while he recovered from the pulsating sensation in his cock.

"Oh!" She moaned and Ricky gave her ass a smack again.

"I'm going to enjoy spanking this ass when you're naughty, Amelia. I'm going to make it pretty and pink. My hand looks so good on your ass, holding it in place while my cock disappears inside of you."

"Oh God, Ricky," Amelia said, tilting her head back, parting her lips, and thrusting back her hips.

Murphy reached up and pinched her nipples, tugging on them as Ricky thrust in and out of her ass, alternating pumps of his hips with smacks to her backside.

Ricky grabbed a hold of her hips as Amelia screamed her release.

"Too fucking good. You're incredible," Ricky said, sounding like his teeth were clenched as he held his cock within her ass and came with a low growl.

Amelia fell against Murphy's chest and he caressed her damp hair from her face. He locked gazes with Ricky, who was breathing heavy. As Ricky slowly pulled from Amelia's ass, he nearly stumbled backward. He grabbed onto her back for support.

"Hot damn, woman. You are a sex goddess. This ass, this body, is fucking incredible. I love you, Amelia. You hear me, Amelia? I fucking love you. I'm never letting you go. Not ever." Ricky leaned down next to her and caressed her cheek as she held his gaze and smiled.

"I love you, too, Ricky," she whispered. Ricky kissed her then caressed her back.

As Ricky stepped away to get dressed, Murphy moved so that Amelia could sit up.

He held her cheeks between the palms of his hand. "This is special, this bond between the five of us. I've waited for you for forever." He kissed her softly.

When he released her lips, she smiled.

"I love you, Amelia. I'm going to take care of you, and so are my brothers."

Amelia smiled, and he could see the tears glistening in her eyes. "I love you, too. I want to feel like this, forever."

He hugged her to him, rolling her to the side as he pulled from her body and snuggled close.

"Close your eyes and rest. We'll shower when the others are done."

She closed her eyes and snuggled against Murphy. He'd never felt so at peace in his life. He'd found his soul mate. He and his brothers found the woman to complete them. What had been a dream, a fantasy that seemed would never come true, became a reality today. He squeezed her tighter. She moaned and pressed harder against him, and he knew she felt the bond between them.

Now if only he could get the aching little fear in his gut to go away. Was he just nervous from taking this chance? His gut never steered him wrong. Something was bothering him, and he needed to figure it out. For now, he would relish in the aftermath of their lovemaking, and the huge step in the right direction toward ultimate happiness.

Chapter 13

After taking showers, Brody was applying some ointment to Amelia's scratches on the back of her thighs. She was naked in front of him as he knelt down on the towel.

She saw his scars on his chest and wondered how he sustained them. "How did you get these?"

He tensed a moment then looked up, his face level with the underside of her breasts and tattoo. "Long story. Battle wounds, ya know?" She felt the sadness in his tone.

Brody placed his hands on her hips, then leaned forward and kissed her belly. The feel of his lips against her skin, and the gentle, intimate way he held her naked body, with such strong and capable hands, aroused her senses. She was lost in the emotions she felt as he explored her skin with lips and tongue.

Closing her eyes, she immersed herself in the feel of his long, thick fingers and his hard palms pressed against her skin. They aroused her, and her pussy clenched.

"What's this?" he asked. She was suddenly pulled from her daze, and the enjoyment of Brody's exploration. She felt his thumb brush across the raised skin, and she knew he was referring to the spot underneath the largest flower of the tattoo. It was the main reason she got the tattoo in the first place. She wanted to forget the pain, and the memory of the time Mano burned her.

He had been smoking a cigar and was pissed at her because he lost a fight. He lost because he wasn't good enough. The other guy was better. It was one of the moments when he proved that he didn't love her and that she needed to break free from him.

As she tried to console him, he freaked on her and pressed the cigar against her side. She remembered the smell of burnt material and flesh. She'd screamed in pain, and he pulled her against him, and kissed her brutally hard. He'd only released her because his brother walked in.

"Amelia?" Brody stood up. He stared down into her eyes and she felt the tears fill them, but she wouldn't cry. Instead, she ran the palms of her hands gently over the scars on Brody's chest and whispered, "I have scars, too."

Her voice cracked and she hugged him to her, keeping the tears at bay as he held her in his arms and cursed under his breath.

"Let's go get dressed and see the others. I miss them so much. Isn't it silly?" she asked, keeping her head against his shoulder. She felt Brody's hands caress her ass and back while he carried her to the bedroom.

"Not silly at all. We're yours now, Amelia, and you're our woman. We'll protect you forever," he said then kissed her.

Amelia hoped that his words were true. But that feeling of uncertainty tinged ever so slightly in her gut. *Life couldn't be so perfect for someone like me. Could it?*

* * * *

When Amelia walked into the room with Brody, Waylon smiled. He walked over toward her, took her hand, and brought her fingers up to his lips. He kissed each digit.

"Come sit down and eat. Murphy and Ricky made some lunch since we missed breakfast."

She smiled, and he noticed the pink blush appear on her cheeks. She was shy and beautiful. He felt his chest tighten. While she was in the other room with Brody, Waylon had expressed his concern over Amelia finding out about his upcoming training and boxing match. Murphy and Ricky ensured him that he needed to be honest and that

Amelia would get the difference. Waylon was a professional fighter, the jerk-off from New York was a fucking joke.

"I need to talk to you about something," Waylon said as Amelia took a seat in one of the chairs around the small kitchen table.

"Okay. What's going on?" she asked then looked at his brothers. They appeared concerned, too.

"You know that I'm a professional fighter?"

She closed her eyes, sighed, then smiled before she opened them. She reached up and took his hand.

"I know the difference. I understand. It will take some getting used to, but I get it."

"Baby, I'm going to be in training the next few weeks. I have a big match coming up to a well-known guy. It's in Vegas, and it's going to be a difficult match. If you can't handle it. If it upsets you, then I won't do it."

He heard his brothers gasp then release angry sighs. Amelia stood up. She reached up and cupped his cheek.

"Waylon, I love you. I would never take away your dreams or stand in the way of your goals. You said that you would never hurt me and I believe you."

He turned and kissed the palm of her hand. Then she sat down.

"So who are you up against?" she asked.

The others brought the sandwiches over to the table and the pitcher of lemonade.

"A heavyweight from Chicago."

She took a sip of lemonade from her glass.

"Not Jerry O'Connor?"

He nodded his head.

"Oh my God, Waylon. You must be really good. He's tough. He's also unconventional."

"Unconventional?" Murphy asked then took a bite of his sandwich.

Waylon leaned back against the counter.

"Yeah. He fights dirty. He has a mean right hook and does these cheap shots. I don't know your style of fighting, Waylon, but Jerry O is a wild one. He has so much pent-up anger in him. I saw him fight over a year ago. His opponent went out on a stretcher. He suffered a major concussion and broken cheekbone."

"Shit," Ricky said aloud.

They were all looking at Waylon.

"I know he's tough. I've got my trainers coming in tomorrow. You think I can't take him, Amelia?" Waylon asked.

She stood up and placed her hands on her hips. "How badly do you want to beat him?"

He looked at his brothers, their stern, hard expressions. It was difficult being so mean and pissed off in front of Amelia, but he was honest.

"I want to win. The grand prize would be a step in the right direction toward retirement."

"You want to stop fighting?" she asked.

"I thought about it." He reached out and gently tugged on a strand of her hair.

"More so recently." He gave a small smile.

Amelia grabbed his hand and held it against her chest as she stared up into Waylon's eyes.

"Don't you dare quit for me, Waylon. This is what you do. This is what has helped you over the years to survive and keep the demons at bay. I won't be an excuse to quit. I won't stand in your way of succeeding. I can help you."

"I'll need you there with me. I'll need you to understand that I'm in training and that I want this."

"You said that the trainers are coming tomorrow?"

He nodded his head.

"Then we better take full advantage of today and tonight to engage in some wild, mind-blowing sex. Because you're cut off, come Monday night."

The guys laughed and Waylon was overwhelmed with emotions and love for this woman before him. He lifted her, she straddled his waist, and he kissed her long and thoroughly. When he finally released her lips while cupping her ass, he smiled.

"Sex with you is an inspiration. And if I can't have this hot, sexy pussy and ass for three weeks, then I'm retiring today."

Amelia laughed then kissed him softly on the lips.

"Let's eat, killer, then we'll go over a game plan. I may be out of work remember? That means I can focus completely on you."

He set her down and gave her ass a smack before she sat down. When he looked at his brothers, they were all smiling and he nearly lost his breath. Amelia did that to them. Amelia was and forever would be their everything.

Chapter 14

Murphy explained the plan to Amelia—lunch at Casper's to get together with some of their military friends and then a quiet dinner alone, at their place, where the beds were king-size and they could share more of themselves with her.

Sitting here now, leaning her back against Murphy's chest and his thighs while he sat on a barstool, made her feel content. She listened to the men joke around a bit and loved seeing them like this. She didn't want to take credit for it, but his friends whispered to her that she was definitely special and thanked her.

Murphy moved his hand to her shoulder then rubbed his thumb up and down along the base of the back of her neck. She had placed her hair in an updo because it was nearly a hundred degrees outside. She wore a light blue sundress, with scalloped edging along the trim and small sequence beading lining the top of the bodice. It was a bit sexy, but Regan had bought it for her, wanting to cheer her up after the Tucker incident.

Her men didn't like the idea of her wearing it in public, but she informed them they she would only wear it when they were around.

She smiled to herself, thinking about how many times Ricky tried to remove it before they left her cottage.

She loved the feel of Murphy's fingers caressing her. He and his brothers always touched her, kept her close to them, and she sought them out every time.

"So, what's the problem you wanted to discuss with us?" Sandman asked then took a slug of beer as he held Murphy's gaze.

His brothers Duke and Big Jay were there as well. Their wife, Grace, had stayed home with the baby. She was feeling tired, being pregnant and all, so they were only staying for an hour. She could tell that these men loved their woman. Every time they said Grace's name, their eyes sparkled.

She wondered if her men would show such love in their eyes, too.

Murphy's hold firmed slightly at Sandman's question.

"I think Amelia should tell you about him." She was shocked. So this was why they came here? They wanted to tell their friends, these men who were all involved with the government and law enforcement, about Mano? Did they really think she couldn't handle this?

She turned toward Murphy. His hand slid down her neck and back to her waist. He gripped her hip bone.

"Murphy, what are you talking about?"

He held her gaze. She was still impressed with his size and muscles. His firm, determined expressions were impressive, and seeing him now, knowing his stubborn, boss-like ways, he wouldn't drop this issue.

"I want you to tell them everything you can about Mano. Where he lives, what he does, what he's gotten in trouble for. I want them to be able to find him and set him straight, so he never bothers you again."

She looked at Sandman, his expression just as firm. He was total military and yet, there was something in his eyes. Something deep and dark that gave her the chills.

As if knowing, he spoke. "Some one wants to hurt you?"

She shook her head.

Murphy gave her hip a squeeze. "Tell him the truth. You can trust him."

She looked at Murphy. "I can't believe that you would do this. I told you that I can handle it. You're not getting involved with this and neither are your friends. He's not going to bother me, Murphy. So what that he calls and texts?"

When the second set of hands landed on her shoulders, she looked back and up toward Brody.

"We think otherwise. Let Sandman do his thing, and if he thinks that this guy will stay in New York, and that he's not a threat, then we'll ease up."

"No, Brody. No." She turned toward the bar, trying to ignore them.

"Let me," she heard Sandman say, and Brody released his hold.

Sandman spoke. "Amelia?"

She looked at him. She clasped her fingers together in nervousness. These men were intimidating.

"Your men are concerned. Why don't you explain the situation to me, and then I can determine if they're just being overprotective."

She thought his statement fair, but she didn't know this guy, despite the way he seemed to show love and affection when he spoke about his wife.

"I don't know you."

He smiled. "No, you don't. But your men do. I can be trusted. Grace was in major danger over a year ago. A serial killer was after her."

"Oh my God." Amelia felt her belly clench. "Well this is nothing like that."

"He hasn't threatened you?"

"Not really. I mean, just saying that things weren't over. That he was giving me time."

"Let him see the text message," Brody interrupted. She held her purse tighter.

"That's an idea. Can I see them?"

She didn't see what harm it could do. He hadn't texted since the night at the club and the Tucker incident.

"It's not really that bad. He'll stop if I ignore him." She pulled out the phone. She slid her finger across the lock pad and saw that she had some text messages and a voice mail. She had left the phone on vibrate.

She would look at them later, but as she pressed the little letter, the latest texts came up and they were from Mano. She swallowed hard.

"What is it? What's wrong?" Brody asked.

She stared at the latest text.

Whomever you're fucking is a dead man. I'll find out. I'll kill him and then I'll kill you.

Sandman gripped her hand as she tried to close the phone and put it back into her bag. She felt Murphy's arm move around her waist as he stood up and looked over her shoulder.

Her heart was pounding in her chest. Where did all this aggression come from? Why did Mano suddenly want her so badly?

Sandman was looking at the cell phone. She looked at Brody, who held her gaze, and she felt Murphy squeezing her tightly.

"What's going on?" Ricky asked, joining them. She locked gazes with him. Concern for all four men gave her an instant headache.

"Amelia, this is a serious threat. Do you understand that?" Sandman asked.

"Fuck. What the hell do the other two say?" Brody asked, as he looked over Sandman's shoulder. They were looking at her phone, and reading the messages.

She pulled from Murphy's embrace.

"Amelia," Waylon said. She turned around toward him.

Waylon reached out and pressed the palm of his hand against her cheek then neck. He cupped her head and stepped closer. She reached up and held on to his wrist and smiled.

"It's nothing, Waylon," she stated.

"That dick contacted her again, Waylon. He threatened her and he threatened us," Murphy said.

"No. They're just words. He doesn't know anything. When he called me that day, I told him that I moved on. He assumed that I meant on to another man. I'll just change my phone number. I've done it before. I'll do it again." She reached for her cell and Sandman held her hand over the phone. He locked gazes with her.

"This is not something to take lightly. First verbal threats, then physical assault."

"Already been there. So I guess he's going backward." She pulled away from Sandman.

"This guy hit you?" Sandman asked her. He was definitely disgusted.

She turned away and looked at Murphy. "Why are you doing this? Why did you bring me here? I trusted you."

She turned to walk away. "I want to leave now."

Ricky grabbed her hand. He brought it against his chest.

"We'll walk outside to get some fresh air." Ricky led her outside. She wouldn't look over her shoulder at the others. She knew they were angry. Those texts were hard to read for her. She couldn't imagine how difficult it was for them. They said that they loved her, but she just wanted to move on. Maybe if she ignored Mano's attempts at pursuing her, he would eventually stop?

* * * *

Ricky pulled her into his arms and hugged her to him. He caressed along her back and inhaled the scent of her perfume.

"You need to calm down and trust us. This guy, he could come here looking for you, and then what?" he whispered against her ear then kissed her skin. She felt tense, but then began to relax the more kisses he would spread.

"I just want to ignore him. There's been too much drama in my life lately. I don't want any more of it."

He pressed his palm firmer against her back, then softly over her ass, before moving back up to her back again.

"Are you scared of him?" he asked.

She seemed surprised as she immediately looked up toward him. His chin was to his chest, and her head was way back to her shoulders.

"Why are you asking me this?"

"It's a simple question, Amelia. Are you scared of him? Does imagining him physically in front of you, scare you?"

She swallowed hard.

She seemed to think about that a moment. Then she nodded her head. He felt his gut clench and his concern grow even deeper. But she needed someone to be calm here.

"Let me share something with you. Something that a lot of people don't know about me. You see, I was on a mission in…well, let's just say, somewhere foreign, and well, I was captured. Fortunately for me, those who captured me were nowhere near their base. Anyway, without getting into too much detail, I escaped. But not before fighting for my life, and getting stabbed multiple times. I was beaten with whips and rope and metal objects. I wanted to die. I survived it. My will to live and move on and see my brothers and my family again helped me get through that. But for years after, I couldn't sleep at night. I would wake up thinking that I was back there again. I was under their control, their abuse, and their torture all over again. My brothers knew what I was going through. They all had their share of pain and faced death head-on. You survived something, too, Amelia. Your own war at home.

"What I'm trying to tell you is that you're not alone, the way you thought you were. You don't have to hide your phone, pretend that Mano's messages and harassment doesn't bother you, out of fear or acting tough. We're here to protect you. We're here to love you and care for you. You're not alone in this world anymore, Amelia. You've filled our empty hearts. You complete each of us. Take the leap of faith. Let us get this guy off your ass. Fight for us. For what the five of us are together, which is perfection."

She clutched him hard, wrapped her arms around him, and held him just as tight as he had been holding her.

"Okay, Ricky. I'll do it. I'll talk to Sandman and I'll let you protect me."

He brushed a strand of hair from her face then placed his palm against her cheek.

"Together. We're a team, together."

She nodded her head and he smiled, for Amelia was now and forever, his everything.

* * * *

Murphy was still upset. Despite Ricky's ability to get her to cooperate, and give information to Sandman, she hadn't said a word to Murphy. He was used to giving orders and to making decisions for everyone. Now Amelia fell into that category as well.

He watched her quietly walk into their kitchen and look around. She smiled at Waylon as he brushed by her, tickling her side.

"Want to go sit out on the back patio for a bit, or would you like the tour?" Brody asked her.

"The tour first. This is a really nice place you guys have. It's big, too."

Brody reached his hand out to walk her toward the living room.

They disappeared and he stared after them.

"What's up with you?" Ricky asked Murphy.

"Nothing."

"Bull fucking shit, nothing. Spit it out," Waylon said, then sat on the barstool while guzzling down a bottle of water.

"I'm just pissed off."

"At the situation? We all are. At least she spoke to Sandman and he can check this asshole out," Ricky said.

"It's not just that. It's how she reacted to me telling Sandman. She was going to just ignore those text messages. She needs to learn to trust us and not to keep things from us."

"Murphy, she didn't know you were going to tell Sandman. She's used to handling things on her own. She'll get used to it. Just give her some slack," Ricky stated.

"No. I'm not giving her slack. I'm in charge here. You three damn well know that I run a tight, organized house and life. I'm the oldest. Looking out for all of you is my job. Amelia is our woman. She comes first. I won't stand here and allow her to think that she can do what she wants."

"Do what I want? What the hell is that supposed to mean, Murphy?" Amelia asked, raising her voice as she entered the hallway to the kitchen along with Brody. Now Brody looked upset.

Murphy stared down at her. "I'm pissed off, Amelia. I don't like being second-guessed. I was trying to protect you back there at Casper's and telling Sandman about Mano."

She walked closer, with her hands on her hips.

"Well maybe you should have told me what your true intentions in going there were. Perhaps if you were forthright, I wouldn't have reacted so strongly. I don't know those men. I never even shared what happened to me with anyone but the four of you. I guess I felt betrayed."

He thought about what she said for a moment.

"So did I. I felt like you didn't trust us to protect you. I thought that you might even consider not telling us when that asshole calls you."

She released an angry gasp then walked closer and shoved her finger into his chest.

"You are such a stubborn, bullheaded, royal pain in the ass. How dare you think for one minute that you can order me around or place me into your own personal troop of soldiers. Because that's what you're doing, Mr. Drill Sergeant. I'm not in the military. I live my life my way and that's it. You want to bump heads some more?"

He stared at her in shock. She had a fire in her that made his cock instantly harden and his temper flare.

"Watch your tone," he told her.

"Or what?"

He reached out, grabbed a hold of her dress over her belly and pulled her against him. Running his fingers through her hair, he cupped her head and descended upon her lips. He kissed her fully, holding her tight as she struggled only momentarily. Then she kissed him back and climbed his body.

Murphy lifted her up and placed her on the kitchen island. He shoved the bodice of her strapless dress down, exposing her braless breasts to his hands. Cupping them, he pulled the nipples, and thrust his cock against her. She pulled from his mouth and ran her fingers through his hair.

They were breathing heavy as he lowered his mouth to her breast.

"Damn it, Murphy," she scolded him while he sucked as much of her right breast into his mouth as he could and sucked hard. She moaned, gripped his head, and thrust her hips forward. Releasing her breast, pulling lightly on her nipple with his teeth, he stared up at her.

"You're in for a hell of a spanking tonight."

"Spanking?" she asked, sounding shocked. But with her lips red and swollen from their hot kiss and her nipples hard as pebbles, he knew she was aroused by the prospect.

"Hell yeah." He bent down, lifted her up over his shoulder, and carried her to the bedroom.

"Put me down. You're crazy, Murphy."

"They don't call him Mad Dog for nothing, Amelia," Ricky teased.

By the time he climbed the stairs, he had maneuvered his fingers under her panties and straight up into her wet cunt.

"You're so wet woman. *So* fucking wet for your spanking."

He pulled his fingers from her cunt. Amelia moaned as he slowly lowered her to the bed. He peeled the dress down her body and off of her. He reached for the panties and she pretended to move back on her elbows, as if escaping.

He grabbed her ankle, pulled her back, then pulled off her panties. "No fucking games, Amelia. You're my woman. I am your man. Get it through your thick skull."

She flipped onto her belly to scramble up the bed. "You're crazy. I am so not allowing you to do that to me."

"I don't recall any of us asking for permission," Brody said. Murphy smiled as he pulled Amelia lower on the bed. His brothers were stripping out of their clothes.

Murphy ran the palms of his hands up and down her ass cheeks.

"Murphy?" Amelia practically moaned, and he pulled her down to the edge of the bed then lowered to his knees.

He pressed his fingers up into her pussy and she moaned aloud.

"So fucking wet. I might not need that lube, Ricky." Murphy leaned forward and licked her cunt where his fingers stroked her.

"Oh God. Oh God, I'm coming." She moaned. He sucked her clit hard and Amelia screamed her first release.

"Give me that." Murphy took the tube of lube from Ricky. He squeezed some out then lifted her by her hips, so that she was on all fours.

He pressed a finger full into her anus.

"Oh. My. God," she said.

"Offer me your ass, Amelia. Offer it to all of us, who love you and are in charge of you."

She wiggled her hips, and Brody lay on his belly next to her and pressed a finger to her pussy.

"Brody, please. Oh please do something."

Murphy smacked her ass and she jerked downward.

"She is so fucking wet, Mad Dog. Go in. You're good to go," Brody said then thrust fingers up into her.

"With pleasure." He pulled his fingers from her ass and gave her cheeks three consecutive smacks.

"Oh!" She moaned aloud.

"Fucking A, baby, you're incredible," Murphy stated. He aligned his cock with her anus and slowly pushed into her. Amelia moaned and widened her legs, trying to allow him entry.

"Nice and easy, honey. Let him in," Ricky said as he caressed her hair from her face. Waylon took position in front of her, kneeling and holding his cock.

"I can't. I need something more. I need…" she said, pleading.

Murphy thrust completely into her ass. He gripped her hips and held himself deep inside of her.

"We know what you need, baby." Waylon stroked her lips with his cock and Amelia opened to accept him.

Murphy watched in admiration as he thrust back and forth into her ass. He gave her ass another two smacks, and Waylon had to grab her hair and head to keep her in place, sucking his cock.

"Fuck, baby, easy now. Go easy on me," Waylon said, closing his eyes and grinding his teeth.

Murphy pulled out and thrust back into her ass.

"Fuck," he said then exploded inside of her.

Brody reached under her and pressed fingers to her cunt. Her body convulsed and Waylon exploded as she orgasmed at the same time.

She pulled her mouth from Waylon, making him fall backward moaning.

"Oh God, I need more." She reached underneath herself and pressed fingers to her cunt.

"Sweet mother, that's fucking hot," Ricky said.

"Fucking incredible," Brody stated then moved underneath her by lifting her up and placing her right onto his shaft. She immediately sought the relief she was looking for. Murphy saw her face as he leaned around to kiss her.

"Ride him good. Fuck him and claim him," Murphy told her and she did just that.

"Give me that lube now," Ricky ordered. Murphy tossed him the tube and a few seconds later, Ricky was behind her, standing at the edge of the bed, aligning his cock with her anus.

Amelia pushed back and Ricky smacked her ass.

"Easy. I don't want to hurt you."

"Get in there now. I want it now." She thrust down on top of Brody. Brody held her hips and thrust upward. "Fuck." He moaned as Ricky shoved into her ass.

Murphy watched in admiration and arousal as Amelia threw her head back, pushed her large breasts out and moaned.

"Yes. Oh please. Please don't stop."

Brody and Ricky continued to take turns thrusting into her. Finally Brody exploded, unable to move anymore. He was obviously overaroused.

Ricky smacked her ass two more times. "You will listen to Murphy. He is the boss of you. He has your best interests at heart." He pumped his hips, wrapped an arm around her midsection, and exploded inside of her. She gasped and her body shook as she came.

"This is totally not fair. You four ganged up on me." She pouted as she lay motionless on Brody's chest.

They each stroked her skin and gently rubbed her ass.

"Apparently you like when we gang up on you," Murphy whispered then squeezed her butt.

"She especially enjoys when we all spank her ass during sex," Ricky added.

"I didn't get to spank her ass," Brody exclaimed.

"I don't think that I did either," Waylon added.

Amelia lifted her head up and looked at them. "Well, the night is young." She lifted up and began to climb off of Brody. Murphy wrapped an arm around her waist then pulled her into a cradle position in his arms.

"Not so fast, little one."

He set her down onto her feet, pulled her into his arms, and kissed her until she was limp.

He would have to learn how to accept Amelia's independence, like she was going to learn to accept his authority. But, a little voice inside his head hoped that every little challenge ended like this one. In the bedroom, making love.

Chapter 15

Amelia's cell phone rang first thing Monday morning. She saw the caller ID with Ricky by her side.

"It's Toby. Probably telling me that I'm fired."

"Answer it and see," Brody whispered from the other side of her. Murphy and Waylon were already up and downstairs. The trainers and Waylon's agent were on their way over to the gym she had yet to see. That would be a whole other thing to face.

Ricky caressed her hip as she sat up.

"Hello."

"Amelia, it's Toby. Are you okay?"

"Yes."

"I heard about what happened. I'm so sorry. If you need a few days off, please take them. We'll cover for you."

"You mean, I still have a job?"

"Why the hell wouldn't you? You were attacked. He could have really hurt you or worse. I know my son. He and I aren't exactly on good terms. I've tried my hardest to get him the help he needs, but he's refused time after time. This was the last straw."

"But, he came to see you at the hospital. You seemed friendly."

"Polite, in front of you. The envelope was money he said he needed to fix his truck, so that he could accept a construction job. Turned out, the money was to support his drug habit. He was high you know, when he attacked you. The police said he was drunk, too. Toxicology reports say heroine. Can you believe that? Please say that you'll come back here. We need you."

"Well, I need the job. I'll be there."

"Well, take a few days. Just be sure to make it to the barbeque next weekend. After all, you're in charge of it and sure did raise a lot of money. The families are going to love it."

"Okay. How about I see you tomorrow."

"Whenever is good for you."

She disconnected the call, closed her eyes, and released a long sigh. "Still have a job?" Brody asked.

"Yes, I do." She explained about Tucker.

"Damn guy needs help," Ricky said as he got up from the bed.

"He does. Maybe I should go in today."

Brody wrapped an arm around her waist and hoisted her backward. He maneuvered over her and between her legs. "Not so fast."

He covered her mouth and kissed her. That kiss grew deeper and soon she was thrusting her hips against his very engorged cock.

He released her lips. "Ricky can make us breakfast, while I teach you a little bit about household rules."

"Household rules?"

"Rule number one, our beds are your beds. Wherever we want to make love to you, you will oblige."

"That sounds like two rules," she teased him then reached down and aligned his cock with her pussy. He lifted up then slowly stroked into her.

"Fuck it then. The rules are, what we say goes, so prepare to be naked and thoroughly loved."

She ran her fingers through his hair as Ricky began to get dressed.

"You know, they should call you something other than Ice. You're so sweet and warm."

Ricky let out a loud laugh.

"Like what?" Brody asked, then thrust into her hard.

"I don't know, but you're not cold as ice. You're as warm and soft as a teddy bear."

"Oh shit. I like that, Amelia. He can be your little teddy bear. How sweet," Ricky teased.

Brody threw a pillow at Ricky then sat up and thrust into Amelia, making her moan.

She grabbed onto his arms.

"Teddy bear, huh? Honey, I'm more like a grizzly." Brody leaned down and nibbled hard against her collarbone. She squealed as he continued to suck and nibble on her sensitive skin as she laughed so hard her belly hurt.

Ricky walked out of the room. "Have fun, Teddy." Then he chuckled.

Amelia laughed as Brody finally stopped tickling her. He eased his cock out then stroked hard into her again.

"I'll get you back you know?"

Amelia smiled, feeling lighthearted and loved as she trailed her finger over one of Brody's nipples. "Don't worry, I'll come up with a super funny nickname for Ricky next."

"Can't wait." Brody lowered over her, taking her hands and clasping their fingers together above her head. With every stroke, she felt his cock reach her womb. Their gazes were locked, as they made love, then came together in one sweet moment of pure bliss.

* * * *

The weeks passed, and Amelia attended the veterans' barbeque along with her men. It had been a complete success. She had met Waylon's trainers and his agent, but she hadn't entered the barn, where his state-of-the-art training gym and boxing ring was located.

Today, dressed in shorts, a tank top, and tennis shoes, she ventured on over there instead of hanging out with Regan and Velma. They had been so supportive of her, and even Elise talked to Amelia about moving on and being such a Godsend to her sons.

She took a deep breath and opened the door. Entering unnoticed, she heard the familiar sounds of boxing gloves striking an object. The boxing ring came into view immediately. Waylon wasn't kidding when he said he had a state-of-the-art training gym in his barn. There were cooling vents coming out of the ceiling, and the surrounding floor was hardwood. Along the sides were various types of boxing bags, workout equipment, treadmills, and bicycles. There was everything a boxer needed to train for the best.

She walked closer and could tell immediately that Waylon was in the ring and wearing black camo shorts. She saw his tattoos, the padding around his head and face, and the professional way his legs and body moved. He looked sharp and capable.

Brody spotted her. He immediately walked away from the ring and the other men surrounding it. She heard Waylon's trainer, Jose, giving him pointers.

"Watch those left hooks. Remember, O'Connor fights dirty. He'll sweep out your feet if he gets the chance."

The other guy in the ring was countering the punches. He was a big guy, too, but not as cut up and defined as Waylon. It had to be Quincy. Him and Diver were part of Waylon's training team. They were very fond of Waylon and his brothers and had joined them a few nights for dinner at the house where she cooked the meals.

Brody took her hand and squeezed it as he brought it to his chest.

He knew she had been scared to come here. Scared to see Waylon box and worried about the emotions it might cause. "You okay?" he asked.

"Yeah. I'm good. This is impressive."

"Yeah, well Waylon really enjoys boxing. He's made a lot of money over the last five years. This fight is a big one."

"I know. Vegas always puts on the big events."

"Have you changed your mind about coming?"

"I'm not sure."

"Well, you have two more days to decide. He's almost finished. Want to come over and get a closer look?"

She shook her head.

"I don't want to distract him."

"He's in his zone. I bet you won't be a distraction, but instead a major support for him."

Amelia wasn't certain, but as Brody brought her closer, she began to focus more on Waylon's form and his counter moves to Quincy.

"That's it. Now, try some cheap shots, Quincy. Go over that move we saw in the video," Jose stated.

She stood to the side next to Brody and Ricky. Ricky caressed her back then ran his hand along her backside. He bent down to whisper into her ear.

"These shorts are kind of short. You better only wear them around the house." He moved his fingers up under the seam to that delicate, sensitive flesh where her ass cheeks met her thighs.

She stared at his chiseled, bare chest. "Well you be sure to wear a shirt, unless you're only around me."

He smiled. "Okay, darling. I promise."

He moved his hand then pushed a finger through one of the loops on her shorts. His hands were so big, that Ricky's palm was splayed across her backside possessively.

Brody now stood behind her and placed a hand on the back of her neck. She was immediately aroused, as usual. But determined to act unaffected.

"No, Waylon. Not like that. He'll catch you. You have to remember who you're dealing with."

Waylon banged his fists at his side.

"What's up with you? Why can't you focus?" Jose asked.

"I'm fucking up my jabs and my hips as I go in for those counter strikes. They feel awkward."

"Well try it like this," Diver suggested as he showed him what he meant. He tried the move again and still got caught in Quincy's right hook under his chin.

"Fuck!" he yelled out.

They repeated a few moves, but they didn't quite feel right to Waylon.

He turned around and saw Amelia standing there with his brothers.

"Hey, what's going on?" he asked. Quincy stepped back and took a breather.

"Do you need a break? Maybe clear your head?" Jose asked.

Waylon nodded. "Let's give him a few minutes, Quincy. Come on down here and let's take a look at that video again. Maybe we can come up with a better counter move," Jose stated as Quincy waved hello to her then walked to the corner of the room where a flat screen TV was set up.

Waylon sat down on the edge of the ring.

"Hey, baby, so what do you think of the place?"

She walked closer with Ricky and Brody following.

"It's impressive. So are your moves. You look great." It was difficult to not drool over the man right now. He was dripping with sweat, but for some reason, it turned her on entirely too much. She actually felt her pussy clench and her nipples harden. She looked away and cleared her throat.

"What's wrong? Something bothering you?" Brody asked Waylon.

"I don't know. I don't like preparing to fight a dirty fighter I guess. This guy is talking so much trash. It's turning into a three-ring circus. I've got all these big shots coming out there to watch, and wannabes, too. Jose's getting calls by companies wanting to sponsor me or pay me to wear their logos and shit or pose for pictures. It's fucking annoying."

"Hey, this comes with the territory. None of that shit ever bothered you before," Ricky told Waylon.

"It's different. I'm getting frustrated with these moves."

"Have you tried not focusing so much on what might happen and just focus on your speed, and compensating for the cheap shots?" Amelia asked.

"What do you mean? You want me to pretend like this guy isn't a street fighter or something?"

She swallowed hard. Waylon was way pissed off.

"Waylon, what made you start fighting?" she asked him.

He looked at his brothers as Jose, Quincy, and Diver approached.

"To keep my mind off the bad shit in my head. To forget about the war and the pain. It helps me to release all my anger and frustration."

"Okay. So what makes you think that street fighting is any different? These men have been battling not only their bad upbringings, their pasts, their faults, and their own ghosts, but all those scars of their own and an opportunity to not feel like a loser. The difference is that some legitimately are looking for a way out and to live in freedom, while the others are looking for the easy way out and will cheat, lie, or rip you right off in front of your face. It comes down to the hunger, Waylon. How hungry are you? How badly do you want to beat Jerry O'Connor?"

He just stared at her a moment.

"How much will you dislike it if I want to continue to fight? If I want to beat Jerry O, and go for the title?"

She hadn't expected that. She looked at the others. Quincy, Jose, and Diver walked toward the other side of the ring to give them some privacy.

She realized that this was what was really bothering Waylon. He had decided to continue a career in fighting and he was basically saying that he would give it up for her.

She stepped closer and placed her hand on his thigh.

"I'm here aren't I, Waylon? I know it took me a while, but now that I'm here and I see your talent, your abilities, I'm with you. If this makes you happy, if this is a dream to achieve, then I'll be right beside you in support. I love you, and the past doesn't matter."

He wrapped his boxing glove arm around her shoulders and pulled her against his sweaty chest.

"I love you, too. That's what I needed to hear."

"Okay, enough mushy stuff," she stated, pushing away from him. "Get your ass back in that ring and focus. Remember, you're a soldier. When Jerry O, throws you a cheap shot, use one of your hand-to-hand combat moves. A striker shot to the neck. If the ref doesn't call his cheap shots, then he won't call your counter ones."

"Hot damn, I think I'm in love," Quincy stated as he stared at Amelia and shook his head. They all laughed.

"Do you want to take back what you just said, before you hop into this ring with me?" Waylon asked.

"Sorry, Amelia. I didn't mean any disrespect," Quincy stated, then bowed in front of her.

They all laughed and Waylon gave her a wink before he stepped back under the ropes and into the ring. From there on out, he looked more relaxed and Amelia felt proud to be his.

Chapter 16

Amelia stood in the hotel room at the MGM Grand. She smoothed out the designer dress Regan and Velma helped to pick out in one of the boutiques downstairs. The men had told them to go shopping, then meet them in the lobby to escort them to their seats. The gown was exceptional. An emerald green, knee-length, snug-fitting dress, with a plunging neckline. It matched the plunging back, that fell very low to her ass. She'd never felt so sexy and exotic in her life, and she hoped that the men would love it.

She stepped into the matching high heels then looked at herself one more time in the mirror.

There was a knock at the door. Glancing at the clock, she knew it had to be Velma and Regan.

She cheeked the peephole, before opening the door.

"Oh my God, you two look incredible," Amelia told them as Velma and Regan sashayed into the room. Velma wore a short, very tight-fitting black-and-purple sequined dress with purple stilettos. Regan wore one in red, her favorite color.

"You look like a model, Amelia. My God, our brothers are going to freak out," Regan stated and Velma high-fived her.

"Hey, you two said that they would love this dress."

"Love taking it off of you," Regan added.

"Not love the men that will be drooling and staring," Velma added.

"Like your men will be any different?" Amelia countered.

"We just left them to come get you. They headed downstairs," Velma said.

"Well then. Let's go. I'm so nervous, I feel like my legs are going to give out." Poor Waylon had been bombarded by reporters and company representatives. He was actually considered an underdog in this fight. Which didn't sit right with Waylon until Amelia had given him another pep talk, as he liked to call them.

She placed the hotel key card into her purse then headed out with Velma and Regan.

As they took the elevator, they discussed the energy of the hotel all weekend and the fights that took place last night. There were a few more fights after Waylon's, but his was all she really cared about.

As they exited the elevator, they indeed caught the attention of many people. But as they walked through the crowd, Amelia stopped dead in her tracks. She gripped Velma and Regan's arms to stop them. Abruptly she turned around and faced the other way.

"What's wrong?" Velma asked. She heard the whistle and gulped.

"Hot damn, woman, you look incredible. What are you doing in Vegas?"

She turned back around, not wanting to scare Velma and Regan.

"Do I know you?" she asked.

Escala gave her an immediately shocked expression.

"Hmm, I thought I knew you, sexy." He nibbled his bottom lip, then looked her over, making her feel gross and violated.

"Who was that?" Regan asked.

"That was Escala. He's involved with the boxing industry on a low scale. He's a nobody, but he's also Mano's brother.

Regan grabbed her arm to stop Amelia from walking.

"He's Mano's brother? Oh fuck, Amelia."

"Please don't say anything. Please, Regan, Velma, just keep this between us. We're going to be with the guys from here on out. Even if Mano is here, he can't get to me or try anything with all the men around us. I don't want Waylon to find out. He needs to focus on this fight. He doesn't need a distraction."

"Okay, okay, Amelia, calm down before you have a heart attack," Regan stated. "We promise, right, Velma?"

"Right. Just be sure to stay with our brothers," Velma said as they continued to walk. Now Amelia was really nervous.

Then they rounded the corner to the lobby, and there was a huge crowd of people waiting to enter and take their seats around the boxing ring.

They heard the whistles. They saw the eyes upon them and then Regan's men found her and Velma's men found Velma. Amelia wondered where Murphy, Brody, and Ricky were.

She felt the hand against the back of her neck and then the large body against her.

"Are you out of your mind wearing something like this, and walking around without one of us?" Murphy whispered.

She turned toward him, instantly happy and relieved to see him. "What is this?" Brody asked then walked around her, checking her out. Ricky grabbed her hand and pulled her to him. He kissed her hard on the mouth, making a scene. Then Brody kissed her and finally Murphy.

"That ought to do it," Brody stated. She knew they did that on purpose, but as she reached for Murphy's hand and faced the crowd of waiting people, she caught sight of Mano, and he gave her the look of death.

* * * *

Murphy leaned over to kiss along Amelia's bare neck. His cock was so fucking hard right now. Sitting in the damn theatre seats was torture. He inhaled her perfume and closed his eyes. "You smell incredible."

She leaned into him as Brody caressed her knee and thigh. Seeing her in the glamorous dress made him feel wild and possessive. Ricky was leaning forward, as he sat behind her and rubbed his thumb back and forth against her neck.

Murphy stared down at the cleavage of the dress. It dipped so damn low, he wondered if the designer made a mistake. It appeared as if her breasts would emerge with the wrong move. "I love this dress, baby, but not all the looks you're getting. You look hot."

She reached up and cupped his cheek.

"I wore this for you and your brothers. Do you think that Waylon will like it?"

"He'll love it," Brody stated.

They watched a few other small fighting matches and then it was Waylon's turn.

As soon as the announcer indicated that it was next, Amelia began to shake.

"Hey, are you okay?" Brody asked her.

"Yes. Just nervous. God, I'm so nervous that I'm shaking," she admitted.

Brody smiled and Murphy patted her knee.

"He'll do fine. He wants this and he's worked hard," Murphy said.

They all cheered when Waylon's name was announced, and his heavyweight championship record. Then there was Jerry O'Connor. The crowd cheered, and then the fight began.

Amelia sat forward in her seat. She watched as if she understood every move and every aspect of boxing. Murphy wasn't surprised at all. They had learned so much about her in the last two months, and they were all impressed.

It was an exciting match. Murphy was on the edge of his seat and Amelia kept grabbing onto his arm, cheering on Waylon and screaming his name. His heart pounded inside of his chest, as he saw the love, the true support and commitment she had toward Waylon and his boxing profession. After everything she had gone through, she put aside her fears, her bad memories of the past, and put Waylon and them first. This was what true love was all about, and nothing could destroy that.

She jumped up along with the rest of the crowd and so did Murphy. He watched as Waylon took a shot to the chin, stumbled backward, and then nearly got his feet swept out from underneath him as O'Connor was notorious for. Next came the cheap shot, but Waylon was ahead of him. He ducked. He sidestepped then came back with a vicious right hook to O'Connor's jaw.

"Keep it up, Waylon. Hit him again. You got him!" Amelia yelled out. "Come on, Sniper, do this. Finish him!" Ricky yelled from behind Amelia.

The crowd was going wild, screaming Waylon's name. O'Connor got pissed and took a few counter shots at Waylon, but Waylon saw them coming. They were going hit for hit. One punch after the next, and countering right hooks, jabs, left hooks, and jabs. It went on and on, and then Waylon took a hit to his cheek as he threw an upper cut to O'Connor's jaw, and that was it. O'Connor fell backward, landing on the ring floor with a thump. Waylon shook his head, kept boxing around as the bell rang. The ref raised his hand signaling that he was the winner and the crowd cheered.

Amelia and Brody hugged one another, and then she hugged Murphy. Ricky was smacking Murphy on the shoulders yelling and cheering for their brother.

"And the winner, by knockout, the new heavyweight champion, Waylon 'Sniper' Haas!" the announcer declared over the microphone, his words as loud as the crowd's cheers.

* * * *

It was such an amazing boxing match. Amelia felt the rush and the pride for Waylon's success after such hard work. She couldn't wait to see him and hold him.

The men escorted them out of the arena. It had taken some time, but Waylon was being interviewed by media and bombarded with excited fans. This was going to be a new and exciting stage in Waylon's life. She smiled to herself. She was so proud of him.

She felt the arms around her waist from behind and Ricky kissing her neck.

"That was amazing. Are you okay?"

She reached up and caressed the palm of her hand against his cheek.

"Very okay." She smiled and he turned his face to kiss her hand.

She looked at Murphy and Brody who flanked her on either side. They were like her personal bodyguards and she couldn't wait to celebrate with them upstairs. But as they headed toward the doors that led to the locker rooms after showing their passes, she realized it was going to be a long night. There were loads of people waiting to see Waylon. This was his time, his moment of success, and she was overwhelmed with emotions of pride and love for him. He'd achieved his dream. He was going to be a huge success.

It took a bit of time before they could see Waylon and then some security came down the hallway where they all waited.

They caught sight of Murphy and he nodded.

"Let's go," he said. The rest of the family and friends waited for them at one of the restaurants and bars in the hotel. They knew that it would be a couple of hours before they saw them and Waylon.

Brody held her hand as the security guards led them to a big, fancy locker room and then sitting area. It was impressive as well. Frankie, Waylon's agent, was there to greet them.

"Can you believe that?" he asked with a huge smile as his cell phone rang.

"I have to take this. Waylon is in the back showering, Amelia. He wanted to see you right away," Frankie stated then headed out toward the other room. He was scheduling interviews and photo ops for

Waylon. She chuckled to herself. Waylon was not going to like that one bit.

"Anyone else need a drink?" Ricky asked, walking over to the full bar and grabbing a cold beer.

Quincy came out of the back room along with Jose and Diver.

They all congratulated them and they hugged and shook hands. Jose kept his hands on her shoulders as he stared down into her eyes.

"You're an amazing woman. He loves you so much, and you helped him to win this fight." He leaned down and kissed her cheek, then released her, and wrapped an arm around Quincy's shoulder. "We'll meet you all outside."

"Go on in, honey. I'm sure he can't wait to see you," Brody said, giving her body the once-over with hunger in his eyes. She walked to the door and entered. There was a short hallway and then another door. As she walked closer, the door opened and there was Waylon. Hair wet, towel wrapped around his waist, and the smell of soap and heat instantly surrounded her.

His eyes widened and a huge smile fell across his face. Then he looked her over.

"What the hell is that you're wearing?"

At first she felt her heart sink, but then realized that they really were very protective of what belonged to them, and she didn't mind being theirs one bit at all. She twirled around then placed her hands on her hips, causing the material to press against her breasts and expose a bit more skin than she intended.

In a flash he stalked toward her wrapped her around the waist and hoisted her up against him.

He cupped her breast and squeezed.

"These belong to me and my brothers only. Now kiss me, woman, before I explode."

She leaned up, and as she parted her lips, Waylon slammed his down against hers. The kiss grew hot and wild in no time at all and soon she was up against the wall, her dress lifted and his fingers were stroking her cunt.

The door opened and she heard the chuckles.

"We'll cover you two," Brody declared then closed the door.

Waylon pulled back and she cupped his cheeks between her hands, looking over the bruised cheekbone.

"You're hurt."

"No. I'm perfect because of you." He stroked her pussy with his fingers and she gripped his forearms. The overwhelming need for him to be inside of her took her breath away.

"Waylon, please."

He kissed along her neck as he pulled his fingers from her pussy and somehow pushed her panties down.

The towel against his waist fell and as she held on to his shoulders, he adjusted his cock to her pussy.

"You complete me, Amelia. I couldn't have done this without you in my life."

He shoved into her slowly and she released a sigh of relief.

"I'm so proud of you, Waylon. You fought hard. I love you, too."

He kissed her again and continued to stroke his cock into her, joining their hearts and bodies, and ultimately sealing the night's fate. He released her lips. They locked gazes and with every stroke, her love for him and for his brothers grew deeper and stronger. Nothing could ever break them apart. Nothing.

* * * *

Murphy, Waylon, Ricky, Brody, and Amelia were walking with their family and friends after the long evening. Waylon was exhausted, but laughing along with his brothers as Amelia, Regan, and Velma walked a few feet ahead of them.

"I can't wait to go to bed. What an emotionally draining night," Regan said and both Amelia and Velma agreed.

They walked between crowds of people, and as Amelia turned to look back at her men in admiration and desire to be with them tonight, she caught sight of Escala.

She stopped, looked at everyone, then heard Regan scream. Then both her and Velma fall backward away from her.

The large thick arm moved around her midsection and the knife pressed lightly against her neck.

Her men's facial expressions turned to fear and anger.

"Let her go!" Murphy yelled.

"I told you that I would come for you, Amelia."

Mano.

She struggled to get free. When she felt the knife cut her skin by her neck, she screamed.

"Don't move or she's dead. I'll fucking slit her throat right here."

In a flash there were police everywhere. Fear and dread filled her heart. She was going to die. After everything she had gone through, Mano was going to win out. She fought for the love of her men, for the new life she had, and to get away from her past, and now this asshole was going to end it all.

"Let me go, Mano. Put down the knife. There's no need for this."

"Shut up, Amelia. You're mine."

He backed her up against the wall and then into the elevator.

"No! Stop there. Put down the knife and this can end right here!" Waylon yelled.

"Fuck you. You'll never have her again. Never."

The doors closed and Mano shoved her against the wall. He looked her over.

"Fucking four men at once? You're a whore. This dress, the makeup and hair, doesn't hide the slut you are." He struck her across the face and she screamed as she nearly fell to the floor. Gripping the metal hand bar she pressed her back against the mirror walls.

He gripped her face and head between his huge hands. Mano was almost as big as Waylon, but only a little over six feet tall. He was a mean son of a bitch. He was covered in badass tattoos and he had no rules. He did what he wanted, when he wanted. She could smell that hard alcohol on his breath, and then she saw his eyes. He was on something other than just alcohol.

She needed to calm him down.

He stared at her lips then moved his hand down and cupped her breast. She grabbed at his wrist and he licked her lips then plunged his tongue into her mouth.

She tried shaking her head side to side to get him to release his hold, but she couldn't. He was so strong. Always so much stronger than her. Her life passed before her eyes. She wouldn't make it out of here alive. Not unless Mano wanted her that way.

He pulled from her mouth then pressed his body against hers. Her spine hit the handrail. She gasped.

"I'm going to take you upstairs to my room and fuck you all night long." She jerked when she heard the click of the large, sharp switchblade open against her ear.

He moved it down her neck to her breast, mere inches from her skin.

"I can leave my mark on you everywhere or anywhere I want. They'll know that you belong to me. I won't let them have you."

The bell went off on the elevator, indicating that they had stopped. She saw the evilness in his eyes, and knew that look. Mano had finally lost his mind. All the drugs, the drinking, the past problems had weighed their toll on him and now he was going to take her with him.

He gripped her arm and pulled her out of the elevator. She struggled to get free.

"No. I won't go with you."

He shoved her hard against the wall, and then struck her again. She shoved at him and felt the cut to her forearm. She screamed and he reached out, gripping her hair and pulling her hard toward him.

Her lip was bleeding and her cheek sore. His evil face was right up against hers. They were nose to nose and she shook with such fear, she thought she might have a heart attack. He stuck his tongue out and licked the blood from her lips.

"Even your blood tastes good."

"Stop! Police!"

She heard the voice and Mano looked back over her shoulder, then wrapped an arm around her waist and turned her so that the police could see he had her and the knife.

In a matter of seconds, the wide hallway was filled with police and her men.

She cried as she saw their faces. Her men were as scared as she felt.

"Put down the knife, and let the woman go. It's over," one man, wearing a suit and holding a gun, stated.

Mano shook his head.

"She's coming with me. I'll kill her right here if I have to."

"No. Don't kill her. Just put down the knife," Murphy yelled.

"Fuck you! You can't have her. She'll never be yours again!" Mano yelled then began backing up. She could tell that the police and her men were panicking. If Mano got her into a hotel room, with the door closed and locked, he could kill her. He could hold her hostage and have his way with her. She wouldn't let him rape her. She would rather die than let this man ever touch her again.

"Mano, please put down the knife. I'll go with you. I promise."

He gripped her harder, making her gasp for air. The knife was by her neck as he used his face to turn her face toward him. He looked down into her eyes. She saw that there was no rational thinking going on in a face and eyes likes his. The evil was overwhelming to see, and her gut clenched, knowing the worse could come of this.

"You'll leave them? You'll come willingly back to me and New York?"

"Yes. Yes, I'll go with you."

He eased the knife down and she turned out of his hold.

"No, Amelia!" Ricky yelled. She froze in place.

Mano reached for her throat. He gripped it hard and she swung at his body, his face. Her nails scratched his face. She could hear yelling and the sound of many footsteps coming toward them.

"If I can't have you, they can't have you."

Mano pulled her toward him and she screamed as the sharp pain hit her ribs and side.

She was shocked.

He stabbed me.

Chaos erupted around her as she fell to the ground, holding her stomach and side. In what felt like slow motion, she looked up and saw Waylon punching Mano and tackling him to the ground. She saw Murphy's wide eyes, the fear, and then Brody's face.

"Lie still, Amelia. Lie still, help is on the way," he said.

She fell back onto the carpeting. Ricky caressed her hair and locked gazes with her.

"He stabbed me," she thought she said aloud but wasn't sure. There was so much yelling. Too many voices, as everything began to move around. Dizziness overtook her.

"I love you," she whispered.

"No, Amelia. You fight Goddamn it. You fight for us. You don't let that asshole win!" Murphy yelled, and she closed her eyes, his face, the last thing she saw before darkness.

* * * *

She was in surgery for hours. They paced the hallways and the waiting room as more friends arrived and then their parents. Everyone was exhausted and had no sleep as fear that Amelia might die ruled their minds.

Ricky looked at his brothers, as the four of them stood alone, by the windows in the waiting area. "I can't believe this is happening."

"She has to make it. It can't end like this. I won't be able to live without her," Waylon stated.

"God, she looked so scared, and there wasn't a Goddamn thing we could do. I never felt so helpless," Brody stated.

"She's a fighter. She's a Goddamn stubborn—" Murphy's voice cracked and he covered his face with his hand. Ricky placed a hand on his shoulder.

"How fucking long until someone gives us an update?" Brody asked.

"Guys. The surgeon is here," their father, Tysen, interrupted.

They hurried inside and listened as the surgeon explained Amelia's condition.

"She's alive."

They all sighed in relief.

"The knife punctured her lung, broke two ribs, and caused some tears in the tissue surrounding the area. Basically, she's rather lucky. If the knife went deeper or a little further to either side, she would be facing other issues. I've repaired what I could and placed a chest tube between her ribs to help release the air when her lung collapsed. She'll need to stay in the hospital for at least a few days, and then we'll remove the tube and see how she does on her own. This is going to be a long recovery for her. She'll be in a lot of pain, but we'll talk more tomorrow. Right now she's in intensive care."

"Can we see her?" Waylon asked.

"Not for a little while and until I'm sure she's stable. She's a very lucky young woman with an obvious desire to live because we nearly lost her on the table twice. I'll keep you posted and the nurse will let you know when you can see her."

"Thank you, Doctor. Thank you so much," Murphy said and shook the doctor's hand. His brothers shook his hand next.

* * * *

"Oh God," Waylon said then ran his hand over his face. His father, Sam, placed an arm around his shoulder as Velma, Regan, and Elise cried while hugging one another.

"She's going to be okay, son. She's strong and determined to be with the four of you. Love like that is special. You treasure her. You hear me. You keep positive and when you see her, you treasure every waking moment together."

Waylon nodded his head, and then looked at his brothers, who acknowledged the emotions and bond they shared.

She was special, and they would get through this and love her for the rest of their lives.

Epilogue

Amelia sat on the lounge chair inside the gym and watched Waylon do his workout. It had been a few months, and a lot of resting. But she was doing well now, and moving around more easily. Last night was the first time in a while she had gotten to make love to her men. They had taken their time. Loved her long and slowly, being conscious of her injuries, although, fully recovered.

She did suffer here and there from some breathing issues, but that was expected. Murphy had taken her to a special plastic surgeon, to ensure that there wouldn't be any scars on her forearm and ribs to remind her of that tragic night. He had done a fantastic job. They weren't completely invisible, but anyone looking would have to look carefully to see the thin lines. They weren't visible to her, so that wasn't a concern.

She watched Waylon in appreciation of his hard work. He had taken some time off to be with her after she was discharged from the hospital. But she insisted that the time to achieve his dreams were then and that his brothers could take care of her while he secured some contracts and did what he did best.

He argued, but she got her way, which was taking the men a bit of time to get used to. She smiled to herself. She sure could use one of their spankings they used to give her. She had been racking up the points, but they weren't budging yet. They were so careful with her. They kissed her every opportunity they got, and showered her with love, gifts, and simply their presence.

She jerked in surprise, when she felt the hands on her shoulders.

"Sorry. I forgot," Murphy whispered then took a seat next to her. He gave her a kiss, and she soon forgot the fear that gripped her slightly, whenever someone approached her from behind.

Ricky and Brody came in next, both kissing her before Ricky took a seat on the other side and Brody approached the boxing ring.

It was strange, but she was most content here, surrounded by her men, and in the training room, of all places.

The memories of her past, the battles she fought and the fights she lost, would remain there where they belonged. In the past, where she had been weaker, alone and struggling to stay alive.

After fighting the greatest fight of all, to live, she knew that there would never be a greater challenge. She wanted to live for her lovers. She wanted to feel Brody's strong arms around her, and enjoy his quiet company. He was such a stern, strong, compassionate man, hidden behind a face of steel, unless she was around. She smiled to herself. To listen and laugh with Ricky, as he tickled her, aroused her senses and made her smile from his jokes and teasing. Especially his naughty bedroom talk and all the crazy things he promised to try with her when she was fully healed. Her belly quivered just thinking about the possibilities. She looked toward Murphy. Her big, wild Mad Dog, who got under her skin and turned her on all in the same moment. He was a force to be reckoned with. A soldier through and through. A man to be proud of and love simply for whom he was and what he stood for.

Then there was Waylon. She fought to live, to see Waylon box another day and achieve his dreams. His desire to become a world heavyweight boxing champion had become her dream. He forced her to face her demons and her ghosts from the past and make her see that life was worth living and there were things worth fighting for.

They each had their pasts and their scars to heal, and they did it together. One unit, one team, one family. And she sure did have a family now. A huge one, and she loved them all so deeply.

So, as she leaned back and listened to the sounds of boxing gloves hitting the bags, trainers encouraging moves, and her men teasing yet supporting their brother, she felt content and at home. This was what life was worth fighting for. The moment of realization, that true love existed, and she had just that. It was true love that connected her heart with Brody's, Waylon's, Ricky's, and Murphy's.

Destiny was what you made of it. Working hard, achieving dreams and goals weren't easy at all. Anything worth fighting for and achieved after such heartache, blood, sweat, and tears was worth it. There was nothing stronger than her love for her men. She would love them for the rest of her life.

THE END

WWW.DIXIELYNNDWYER.COM

ABOUT THE AUTHOR

People seem to be more interested in my name than where I get my ideas for my stories from. So I might as well share the story behind my name with all my readers.

My momma was born and raised in New Orleans. At the age of twenty, she met and fell in love with an Irishman named Patrick Riley Dwyer. Needless to say, the family was a bit taken aback by this as they hoped she would marry a family friend. It was a modern day arranged marriage kind of thing and my momma downright refused.

Being that my momma's families were descendants of the original English speaking Southerners, they wanted the family blood line to stay pure. They were wealthy and my father's family was poor.

Despite attempts by my grandpapa to make Patrick leave and destroy the love between them, my parents married. They recently celebrated their sixtieth wedding anniversary.

I am one of six children born to Patrick and Lynn Dwyer. I am a combination of both Irish and a true Southern belle. With a name like Dixie Lynn Dwyer it's no wonder why people are curious about my name.

Just as my parents had a love story of their own, I grew up intrigued by the lifestyles of others. My imagination as well as my need to stray from the straight and narrow made me into the woman I am today.

For all titles by Dixie Lynn Dwyer, please visit
www.bookstrand.com/dixie-lynn-dwyer

Siren Publishing, Inc.
www.SirenPublishing.com

Lightning Source UK Ltd.
Milton Keynes UK
UKHW02f1456020518
321990UK00005B/702/P